PAJAMA PARTY

THE STORY

Also by E. C. Jackson

A Gateway to Hope
A Living Hope

PAJAMA PARTY

THE STORY

a novel

E. C. Jackson

ISBN: 978-0-9961812-9-7

Editing: amberbarryeditor.com and angela.trent@sbcglobal.net
Cover design: FormattingExperts.com
Typesetting: FormattingExperts.com
Book blurb: angela.trent@sbcglobal.net

The Write Way – A Real Slice of Life:
ecjacksonauthor.wordpress.com
Author Page: facebook.com/ecjacksonauthor
Designed by Standoutbooks

Acknowledgments

My third book is complete, and I can happily say I enjoyed writing my first teen and young adult book. God put the idea on my heart to write *Pajama Party: The Story* as a companion to *A Living Hope*, the second book of the hope-themed series. Sadie Cummings, the main character of *A Living Hope*, wrote *Pajama Party: The Story* for the girls of Shiatown.

God graciously gave me the idea, and held my hand during the entire process, as I adapted the play I wrote into a novel. My family, friends, church family, and co-workers were so full of encouragement. I am blessed.

My editors and the formatter, whose company also designed the book cover, provided much needed support and guidance along the journey.

Our hope is that you enjoy reading this story as much as we loved making the story available to you.

A song of David

The LORD is my shepherd.
I will always have everything I need.
He gives me green pastures to lie in.
He leads me by calm pools of water.
He restores my strength.
He leads me on right paths to show that he is good.
Even if I walk through a valley as dark as the grave,
I will not be afraid of any danger, because you are with me.
Your rod and staff comfort me.
You prepared a meal for me in front of my enemies.
You welcomed me as an honored guest.
My cup is full and spilling over.
Your goodness and mercy will be with me all my life,
and I will live in the LORD'S house a long, long time.

Psalm 23
Easy-to-Read Version (ERV)

Chapter One

Sixteen-year-old Karen Duncan entered the guest bedroom on the first floor of her house. Her gaze swiftly swept around the large space. The room hadn't changed since she'd checked it out that morning. This time, the bed lured her to stretch out across it for a nap. She'd had a rough day at school, and the walk home had depleted her energy reserve. Some friends had argued with her outside of the school's office. Their objections to being excluded from her sleepover had turned insulting.

Their harassment sealed the deal for Karen. Not including any of them to spend the night had been the right decision after all.

Besides, she'd received orders to reduce her guest list for the party. An ultimatum from her mom: "Either invite eight girls or less, or no one." Her mother refused to fill their house with more than nine teenagers overnight.

So, Annette set the guest-list limitations, and Karen wisely accepted her mother's decision. It was either agree or call the sleepover off altogether. She didn't want to even think about cancelling the party.

Oh well. Just like me, all my friends need to make changes—even the ones not invited.

She glanced at the silent girl who stood beside her, then beckoned Diane to follow her inside the room. "Go to the family room after you change your clothes."

The blond-haired girl set a suitcase on the floor. Her light-brown eyes scanned the room. "Ooh, I'm so happy to be here. I get stuck at home on weekends unless I hang out with you."

"No way. We rarely get together on weekends. What do you normally do at home?"

"Hole up in my bedroom reading romance novels. I have a very large collection. You can borrow them if you like. I either hang out with you or I stay at home."

Saddened by the thought, Karen gave Diane a sympathetic smile. "Okay, I'll change clothes, talk to my mom, then join you later. It won't take me long. Do whatever you like in the meantime. As my mom says, make yourself at home."

Karen left the room and plodded up the stairs. She stopped outside her parents' bedroom at the far end of the hall. Quickly knocking on the double door, she entered the room without an invitation.

"I'm home, Mom. Diane is changing clothes in the guest bedroom."

Annette Duncan replaced the telephone receiver on the hook before looking up. "Good. I just talked to your grandmother. She sends her love and good wishes for your party tonight."

"I miss Grandma. Can't wait to visit Chicago next spring." Karen rubbed her hands together. "Let's take her and Grandpa to Florida during the summer. I think they'll love it."

Faint lines crinkled around Annette's eyes as she smiled. "That sounds like a dream vacation for you, my dear." She strolled across the room, opened the curtains and sat in a chair by the window. "Are all of the girls you invited coming over? What's the itinerary for tonight?"

Karen beamed. "Nothing's written in concrete, *but*, I bought a noisy interaction game for us to play. We'll use the karaoke machine too. This will be a spontaneous night for us. My thoughts are to just let things happen."

"Then our thoughts are far apart. Your friends are a tad dramatic. Reign them in so I won't have to."

"Mom, you just destroyed my happy list. I want spontaneity to rule tonight."

"If it does I'm sending everyone home early. You're too old to pout. Put that lip back in before I ground you."

"It's my party night. Let me have my own way for once."

"That happened when I agreed to house nine teenagers under my roof tonight."

Karen laughed. "Nine teenagers? You included me in your list."

The war of wills ended when her mother answered the ringing telephone.

While she talked Karen's mind sought ways to sidestep these latest restrictions. She wanted to follow her original plans, and yet still obey.

Snagged by the boundaries set by her mother, Karen conjured up ideas to get her way. She quickly abandoned those thoughts and considered the pluses for tonight. One big one was her younger brother spending the night with a friend. Her older sister had a term paper due on Monday. Brenda planned to spend the weekend writing it. Only her parents might invade their territory tonight. Her mom always welcomed their friends, and made each one feel at home. So did her father. But lately, Karen felt uneasy whenever he came around.

Last spring he had practically destroyed their family with one admission. Sixteen years ago, he'd had an affair with her mother's best friend. What sane person wouldn't feel awkward around a father like him? Months later, Karen failed to warm up to the father who broke her heart. She'd never chosen one parent over the other one, and she didn't play the favorite game with her family. That she once enjoyed spending time with both parents together made the current situation messy. Now she discovered firsthand how learning the truth could disrupt lives.

Sometimes, forever.

In January, Peggy, her mom's best friend since high school, had moved across the country. Two months after leaving Shiatown, she felt compelled to make a confession in a letter.

Karen's mother had quickly left the house and confronted her father at his job. Instead of admitting the truth, her father had denied it ever happened. But later, he was forced to confess, once the friend supplied details he couldn't refute.

Karen had cried when her mother revealed she'd never suspected a thing.

However, her mom, raised in the church, had the forgiveness discussion with each of her children that summer. Too bad her father had never attended church as a child. Maybe he would've behaved differently if he had.

She studied the woman speaking over the phone in a soft voice. Annette had taught her children about God. Yet the family only attended church on special occasions when Karen was younger. The Duncans sat in church on Christmas, Easter, baptisms, weddings, and unfortunately, the occasional funeral. Otherwise, Karen had only gone to church if she spent Saturday night at her cousin's house.

Once her parents' relationship went south, however, her mother rushed into the church doors. She dragged her children with her. Annette quickly rebuilt lost relationships that had long been forgotten. Now she spoke reverently about the God she'd seldom acknowledged.

Karen hated hypocrisy and questioned her mom's sudden enthusiasm for all things God. One day, she voiced her concerns to her aunt, but her aunt replied, "Better late than never." The response had seemed like a scripted reply to a serious query. Now the answer made sense to her. Going to church had opened up a new world for the Duncans.

Annette had never given up on her family. She had worked overtime to keep them all together inside the same house. Her resolve never lessened to preserve their family life. She even made it better, saying, "The hope placed in my heart by a faithful Savior keeps me from falling apart."

That one remark inspired Karen. She'd always considered her mother too passive and her father very strong. But the confrontation last spring revealed the truth. Annette never groveled at her husband's feet.

When the circumstance called for action, Annette fought for her marriage, for their family. She never mentioned the word divorce or covered up her husband's deceit. Her mother confronted him and the friend, and she spoke candidly to her children.

The affair had long passed, but the Duncan family experienced the result as if the betrayal had happened that day. Sam's cheating on Annette, after five years of marriage, made Karen want to scream. Only her mother's false friendship with Peggy had served a great purpose. It helped Karen to break an unhealthy tie with her group of friends. Some friendships lost their appeal after she learned about her mother's friend's deception.

Sam's involvement with another woman added to her sorrow. It upset Karen that her father came down hard on his children when he had behaved worse than they ever had. His failure made previous interactions with him more objectionable. He was far from perfect. Her mind filled with the countless times he'd warned them, "You'll pay full price for the mistakes you make. Don't expect your mother and me to bail you out of difficulties you bring on yourself. I practice tough love."

Karen got tired of hearing him say it.

Too bad you failed to practice the same tough love on yourself. You lied instead of admitting the truth about the affair when Mom confronted you. You've punished us for leaving out minor details about things that didn't even matter.

Family members on both sides had defended Sam. Karen's uncle, her mother's older brother, had supported his cheating brother-in-law. He thought two factors caused Sam to lie once his wife confronted him. Annette's surprise attack at his job unsettled Sam, while the fear of losing his wife sixteen years after the affair ended overwhelmed him.

Her uncle's opinion disappointed Karen. Her father had never been that understanding with his children whenever they made a mistake.

Before the summer ended, her mother and brother accepted him without reservations. However, her sister said, "Mom didn't know about him and the *friend*. Who else is he sleeping with without her knowledge?"

Unfair?

Maybe.

But Karen agreed with her sister's assessment.

Who else, indeed?

His affair had been an unforgettable experience for her. What kind of husband chose to have an affair with his wife's best friend?

Sorry, Mom, but I hope he stays away tonight and skips the loving father and husband routine.

Grudgingly, Karen admitted Sam actually was a loving husband and father. To think otherwise misrepresented his character, but it was the best reason she could come up with for the moment.

Annette hung up the phone and walked Karen toward the door. "You should have left while I chatted with your aunt. I didn't intend for you to hang around. Don't forget your friend is downstairs."

Karen hugged her mom then asked about her day. Her mother deserved both respect *and* attention.

"My day went pretty much as usual. I did some heavy lifting for you downstairs in the family room."

Annette touched her daughter's arm at the door. "About this evening … you're bringing girls together with hopes that they'll become friends. Remember, you can't control other people's lives." She brushed a thumb over Karen's cheek and smiled when her daughter sighed. "I nearly lost my precious girl last May. Don't wage any more winless battles."

"Mom, I'm okay." She hated any thoughts that related to that Saturday.

Her fingers rubbed across her eyelids, and then she blinked at her mother. "Let's not talk about that anymore. It hadn't happened to me before, and it will never happen again. I promise. I'm okay."

"I respect positive thinking, yet knowing why it happened would make me feel better." She lifted Karen's chin with her thumb. "You are special to this family. We need you healthy and strong. Don't take up any more causes too big for you to handle. You have fun at parties. You can't tame the world to your beliefs. Keep your expectations simple tonight. I mean what I say, babe. Have fun. I'll stop the partying if you overreach."

Karen pulled on her bottom lip. Her mother didn't understand what this pajama party represented. It proved that she could be her own person and do the right thing, even if no one else did. Now, her mother's concerns might squash any spontaneity that developed during the evening. Karen needed the freedom to follow her heart wherever it led.

Chapter Two

Karen shut the door to her mother's bedroom behind her. She rushed down the hallway to her room to grab a robe before a quick shower. That was an option she should've offered to Diane.

Hopefully Diane knows she can take a shower if she wants to.

She stood in the doorway to her bedroom pleased with what she saw. Karen loved the room that she and her mom had decorated for her twelfth birthday. No matter how much her sister teased her about the youthful space, Karen refused to change a thing. How could she? Time stood still around her just by being there. Too bad the peacefulness never lasted long enough to make a real difference.

She breathed deeply, grabbed a robe, and headed next door to the bathroom. She felt anxious about the sleepover that night. For the first time in her life the popular sophomore stressed over her plans at the last moment. What had sounded like a good idea three weeks earlier had shaken her up today. She stared into the mirror and rubbed her hands together while she rethought her strategy.

Karen tangled her fingers through the natural hairstyle she loved to wear. She needed a trim. Her locks practically engulfed the elfin features of her face. Was it too late to make a hair appointment for tomorrow afternoon?

Thoughts of getting her hair done failed to lighten her mood.

She had genuine fears about tonight's outcome, and she couldn't push them away. The mismatched group she'd invited could disrupt her somewhat-perfect life. Hopes of making it even better had sparked the sleepover idea.

She wanted to pursue new relationships without losing her closest friends. That didn't include their entire group, either. It just included three of the girls in the group who were invited tonight. They were the girls she felt most comfortable around, even though lately they disagreed on matters that were important to her. What if her friends cast her aside? What if they rejected the new and improved version of herself?

Surely that'll never happen. Yet, sometimes, reality doesn't match my dreams.

Karen hated change.

Real or imagined.

She took off her clothes and got into the shower. The water was warm and comforting. Tension seeped from her body. Karen loved the way the spray trickled over her skin. She would've happily stayed in this exact spot all evening.

Out of the shower, she recalled her mother's lifeless eyes, after she found out about the affair. That sad expression had haunted the house for weeks. That was her father's fault. She sighed. Forgiving an offense proved easier than forgetting it had happened.

Back inside her bedroom, she stepped into the closet and looked for something to wear. She squeezed her eyelids together. Thoughts of the potential problems of the evening assaulted her mind. She might lose all of her friends if her plan failed. What if they ended up hating each other more than ever? Trouble waited to trip her up on every side. Maybe her mom was right. Maybe she was overreaching. Had she messed up by asking Diane to help her set up for the pajama party? Lisa had been livid when she'd spotted the pair lugging Diane's gear home from school. She'd had an angry expression on her face that Karen couldn't mistake, even from a fair distance away.

Karen and Lisa had been inseparable since kindergarten. Only recently, Karen imagined a happy life without her best friend beside her, a possibility she hadn't considered until three weeks ago. In the past, she never made major decisions without asking Lisa's advice. Yet Lisa had chosen the wrong boyfriend in middle school and still dated the boy she should've dumped. Funny how Karen had previously sought guidance from people messing up their own lives. But not anymore. Those days were gone forever. Each day the possibilities of building her future seemed endless. New experiences waited to be discovered.

Life may surpass her wildest dreams *if* she handled tonight the right way. Most of the girls in their group hated the changes Karen made to improve herself. So she was happy she'd only invited three of them to the party. They would probably kick her out of the clique if the girls invited tonight became angry with her, too. She didn't mind saying goodbye to the gang, but she didn't want to lose friendship with the girls coming tonight. Karen didn't want to be rejected, but she also wanted to do the right thing.

A knock sounded on her bedroom door. "Come in, Diane." She grabbed an outfit off the hanger in her closet. Hastily pulling on her clothes, Karen re-entered the bedroom just as Diane scooted inside the door. She wore the same sweatpants and hoodie she had at school.

She grinned at Karen then looked around the room.

"Oh my goodness!" Diane ran across the space and lifted two enormous stuffed honey bears that leaned in a corner of the room.

"I love these bears. You said they were gorgeous, and they are. I'm always at your house—I can't believe this is the first time I've seen your bedroom. It's cute, sort of old-schoolish." Diane kissed the stuffed animals then put them back into their spots. "Is it okay to take a shower? I feel gritty after running in gym."

"Sure, sorry, Diane, I should've offered. Use the bathroom on the first floor. The towels are in the linen closet. Do you need body wash? I have loads of fruity scents."

"Nope. I have some. Thanks. Karen, I like it when your smile reaches your eyes. What are you thinking about?"

"Our special friendship. Thanks for coming over early. Now, why are *you* smiling?"

Diane hesitated at the door. "I like it when you say we're friends. It's shower time. See ya." She waved and left the room.

Once her friend shut the door, Karen's thoughts shifted back to the sleepover.

She's happy. I think I nailed it. It's a win.

Tonight was Karen's attempt to correct a huge error: ignoring anyone she disagreed with. Karen's friends' attitudes were just as off the mark as hers had been, but did she have the right to set her standards for their lives? What happened to her last spring proved she didn't have all the answers. Her friends only thought they knew her both inside and out. How could they really know a person who failed to understand herself? Fooling her peers into thinking she had all the answers to life's problems was terrible. But self-deception was far worse.

Since seventh grade, her selfish behavior had offended many people. She couldn't fix the mistakes of a lifetime in one night, but she could get started. That was why Karen invited two very different girls from her current group of friends. Linda had been a close friend of Karen's in elementary school, while Evette was the type of girl Karen had often overlooked. Both of them were girls who most of her friends ignored. Until recently, she'd run away from what both girls represented, too, although she couldn't pinpoint what that was. But that was her past. Her thoughts were different these days.

Her cousin Sandy thought the sleepover was a good idea. Hopefully, adding one of Sandy's closest friends had stacked the deck in Karen's favor. Only time would tell if that particular gamble might pay off. For tonight, the new and improved Karen Duncan cast aside half of her crowd for a new coalition. Nice word, "coalition." Sometimes paying attention in history class worked.

Even if it made her an outcast at school, Karen was sticking with the original plan. What else could she do? Somehow she must turn her life around. For fifteen years, she basked inside the fantasyland that her parents had created. But that charade ended when she learned about her dad's affair.

Occasionally, painful situations brought about necessary changes. But was it a mistake to bring girls together who only spoke to one another out of necessity, if at all? Karen refused to let the thought gain traction. Negative ideas kept her from making positive changes. What will this new pathway add to her life? Pain as well as hope, it seemed. Odd how something good could also bring discomfort. Strangely, Karen knew what to do next. She must pay attention to her choices. No more tiptoeing over glitches, just letting life happen.

She eyed her reflection in the dresser mirror. Her coffee-colored complexion was blemish-free despite her lack of a cleansing routine. She studied her face. The expression she saw boggled her mind. How could any person have hope-filled eyes with droopy lips?

Oh boy. Is this an indication of what my night will be like? Hmm, it's too late to call it off, nor do I want to.

Her watch proved that time never stopped. She'd just spent the last thirty minutes rehashing her life's story to herself as if she wasn't living it. Seven of her peers would arrive within three hours. Surely Diane had finished her shower. She sighed and then giggled when her eyes twinkled back at her.

Karen bent her body from side to side. It was her ritual just before embarking on physical activity. There might be more furniture to clear out of the family room for the night's fun.

I hope I'm right and that everyone will enjoy themselves.

After a quick glance in the mirror again, she twisted her hair into a knot and tied a sky-blue bandana around her forehead. Her worried expression bothered Karen. Still, she darted down the staircase.

Pajama party, here I come!

Chapter Three

At the family room, she lingered in the doorway. The excitement she felt on the stairs had slipped away. Then her eyes focused on Diane. Her back was to the door. She lounged on the floor with hunched shoulders, sorting through the DVD collection.

Karen looked around the open space before she sprawled onto the floor beside her.

"I'm glad my mom cleared out the furniture for us. Now we can bring in the fun stuff for later."

Diane's shoulders relaxed and her lips broke into a smile. "My mother would never make anything that easy for me." She shook her head as if erasing the thought from her mind. She plumped up a pillow. "Aw, my home until tomorrow."

"That's one way to look at it." Karen rested her head on her arm, and then she sat up quickly. "I like that outfit. Where did you buy it?"

"At a specialty shop in Tulsa. My Mom took me shopping last Sunday." Diane knitted her eyebrows into a single line. She sat upright and rubbed her earlobe. "What time will the others get here?"

Karen sought a diversion from the topic they'd discussed on the walk home from school. She scooted across the floor and replaced the abandoned DVD case back inside the cabinet. "Between six and seven-thirty." She slid back to the spot she'd left.

"That gives us plenty of time to prepare the house before they come. Do you want to work or eat first?"

Diane parted her lips several times before she spoke. "I'm hungry, so let's eat first. Now, back to your friends. Too bad they had meetings after school today or they would be here already. Who ever heard of having meetings on a Friday."

That's why I chose tonight for my sleepover. I wanted you to help me. Alone.

"They'll get here later. Which will give us more time to cook. This way, everyone will eat without complaining. That is ..." Karen stifled laughter, "until they taste the first bite." She touched Diane's arm when the girl didn't laugh. "Don't worry. They'll straggle in once the food is ready."

The quiet girl rose to her knees. "Who's bringing your cousin?"

Karen remembered the walk home from school again. She thought they'd exhausted the who question before they reached her house. Still, she couldn't ignore the inquiry altogether. Especially when her friend's puppy eyes filled with tears. The girl really knew how to get her own way.

Time to find an answer she'll finally accept. Um ...

"Probably Angie. If not, either Sandy's brother or sister will bring her."

Diane nodded but she didn't appear to like the answer. "Was it your idea or Linda's to invite Evette tonight?"

"Mine, but Linda's offer to bring Evette made it sweeter. That makes me happy."

"You think it's nice, but I'm surprised. Linda and Evette have nothing in common. They're coming together? In the same car?"

"Sure, they have plenty of things in common. We're all alike once you think about it."

Karen regretted the quick response. They were not alike. Diane was a loner who hated to spend time alone. That fact had been confided to her last year after a class meeting. The revelation had floored Karen, and she began eating lunch with Diane the very next day. It marked the beginning of a wonderful relationship that grew stronger.

It took her a while to grasp Diane's unpopularity. Jealousy proved to be the culprit. Teachers loved the girl's zest for knowledge and afforded her special treatment. Also, the fact that she was pretty, smart, and considerate fed the green-eyed monster in some people. Diane had only one fault that Karen could see: She tried too hard to be accepted by her peers.

Karen knew the feeling. Being unhappy at home and school, yet happy at the community center and church, kept her off-balance. Sometimes it made her too tired to try new things. Her ideas were too chaotic to act upon. Was that Diane's problem? *Like peas in a pod, we are all so much alike yet still divided.*

"Besides, Evette needed a ride. How can Linda bring her, if not in the same car?"

"You're joking, but they're opposites, just like me and the rest of your friends. Evette keeps to herself and Linda is *way* out there. Nope, believe me, she's hardly Linda's type."

"So say you. Hey, yesterday I heard Joann speak to Linda when the gang passed by her in the hall. How about that?"

"Please. Lisa hugged Linda in the cafeteria the day before, and Joann follows wherever Lisa leads."

"Unless she doesn't want to go there. Trust me, Joann makes up her own mind on important issues. Lisa's hugging Linda was a good thing. Right?"

Diane stood and roamed about the room, then swung around to Karen. "It depends on the reason why she did it. Okay, what's the plan after we all stare at each other for awhile? Instant friendship?"

Karen watched her wander around the space in circles until

Diane called over her shoulder, "Speaking of your *best friend,* what time is Lisa coming? Who's bringing Kathy?"

"Joann. No, I don't know what time they're coming. I would tell you if I knew the answer."

"Oh." Her flat tone reflected disbelief. She sauntered to a stack of magazines and thumbed through the pages without focusing on any one. "I give up on trying to figure out this whole thing. It is what it is. What's for dinner?"

Finally, an easy query. "I know it's cold outside, but I'd planned to grill hot link sausages and hamburgers. Let's eat a taco salad for now. My mom said to play chef tonight."

Diane cast the magazine aside then folded her arms across her chest. "Hmm, your mom's the best. Wish she was my mom. Can I move in?" The teasing voice belied the serious expression on her face. "You're lucky to have her." She flinched as if she'd said too much. Still silent, Diane studied a spot on the wall across the room.

"Stop saying that. I'm blessed, not lucky."

"Blessed? I've noticed something about you. You've been sending mixed signals lately. Talking different, acting friendly with other students, yet hanging out with the same crowd. I'm not complaining. I like the changes. Lose the gang and you'll be perfect."

"Good, someone finally noticed the changes I've made all summer. I talk different because I *am* different. I see situations without the old smoke screens. The haze is gone. Believe me, blessings surpass luck."

"What's the difference? It sounds the same to me."

"Uh-uh, luck implies chance, like something just cropped up. But, as we learned in our physics class, there's a cause for every occurrence. God is the catalyst behind all things good."

Like forming new attitudes and fresh ideas. You have to love yourself so you can love others. Then you can respect people, and treat folks special. Every life counts for something better than being laughed at. No more making myself feel superior at someone else's expense.

"God, huh? You've mentioned Him a lot." Diane replaced the magazine on the rack and snapped her fingers. "You zoned out, like you stopped breathing."

Karen laughed. "You won't get rid of me that easily. I was thinking about the friends I couldn't invite to the party."

"Well, I heard the chatter. You are definitely on the hit list, girl." Diane nibbled her bottom lip. "Where is Lisa? She's home from school by now and lives around the corner from you. Why isn't she here already?"

Surprised by the questions, Karen stared at her. She tried to understand how Diane felt. "Maybe she had something else to do."

The girls coming over were her friends and not Diane's. Sure, Karen would hate to have the gang turn against her, but she had plenty of friends outside that crowd. Diane, her new church buddies, plus, her longtime pals at the community center. After three years, she still loved taking drama lessons there.

Lately, Karen had more in common with the drama club than with her old gang. But Diane didn't have a group of friends to hang out with. She searched for ways to fit in, to belong somewhere. The realization hit Karen hard. How could she have been so insensitive to a friend's needs? Maybe she should've invited a few folks over to play games this evening. Let everyone have fun then have the pajama party next weekend. That would've made a good start, instead of hitting her with everyone at once. Full of remorse, she pulled Diane to her feet and placed an arm around her shoulder.

Her friend leaned against her. "You know that Lisa constantly picks on me. Tonight, I'll be stuck in this room while everyone laughs at her jokes. I think about her insults long after they stop."

"That won't happen this time. Lisa's already promised to behave herself tonight."

Surprise sprang into Diane's eyes as she pulled away from Karen. "Oh no!" She moved across the room until she stood inside the doorway. "Why did you discuss me with Lisa? Everyone will think I cry to you for help."

Speechless, Karen searched for the right words. She'd never seen Diane upset before.

Was telling Lisa to behave herself the wrong thing to do? I was trying to make it go easier for Diane.

"Hey, calm down. It was just Lisa and me. No one else was there. I talked to Lisa to make sure this pajama party succeeded. I can't—"

"You've lost me. How can a sleepover be a failure even with your crowd? You're keeping secrets. What are you hiding?"

"Forget it. Let's fix our taco salad then set up for the party. It's too cold outside to grill. I've decided to boil the hot link sausages instead of grilling meat."

"Okay. I'll let you off the hook this time, but I expected to eat hamburgers too."

"Hamburgers are still on the menu."

Karen was glad the girl relented so easily. She honestly didn't know what to say. No one could explain another person's bad behavior. It was hard enough to explain her own.

"Wait, you're boiling the hamburgers? Ew, that sounds nasty."

"No, no, we're frying the hamburgers. I'm tired. Let's keep it simple."

That way my father won't have to make the fire in the fire pit for us. Then maybe he'll stay away.

Diane followed Karen down the hall. "Me too. Tired, that

is. But, let's grill both the hot link sausages and the hamburgers outside. Why give your friends something else to complain about?"

Chapter Four

While Karen led the way to the kitchen, she recalled one of the main reasons for having the pajama party. Linda Ferguson, the old friend she'd badly mistreated. If she and Linda became friends again, everything else would be simple. After that, the rest of her hope list should fall into place. The goal was to redeem herself with the people she had abandoned. It had been a mistake to replace her old friends with girls she didn't even like.

She wanted the old Karen back. The person who respected her friends and treated them well. Except for Linda, the other girls had moved away, but Karen still remembered their hurt expressions, even now. How could she have been so insensitive?

Her agenda was enormous, but it had to work. Each girl she'd invited had an opportunity to form new relationships. Plus, being honest with each other might help to change their views on lots of topics. That very thing sometimes happened to Karen. A talk with her cousin Sandy usually set Karen straight.

To be a blessing and be blessed. What could be simpler than that? I'm finally doing the right thing for the right reasons. Tonight is going to be fine for everybody. It has to be.

Karen bit off a fingernail tip then snatched her hand away from her mouth. She blinked her eyes to clear her thoughts, and sauntered around the kitchen, removing utensils from the drawer.

Fifteen minutes later, Annette entered the room, just as Diane sat at the table to eat.

"Hello, Diane. I'm glad you were able to join the girls tonight."

Diane pulled out the chair next to her. "Hi, Mrs. Duncan. I hope you're eating with us."

"I will if my daughter agrees." She pointed to the seat. "May I join you?" she asked politely.

Karen set a pitcher of lemonade on the table then sat down. "Mom, please. You don't even need to ask. Grab a seat."

Her mother poured herself a drink while she listened to the girls slam their civics instructor. Next, they blasted teachers in general, particularly the ones piling on the homework.

Karen set her glass down. "It's true, Mom. Teachers give us a ridiculous amount of homework."

Annette had laughed when Diane claimed the heavy workload disrupted her social life. Her smile vanished. "Here's a tip. The purpose of going to school is to learn. Work on your social life over the weekend. I followed that routine. It worked for me, as it will for you. Family time rules after school. Nurture the relationships destined to shape your lives."

The girls' rebuttals to that comment came quickly, and Annette skillfully opposed each one. She finished eating, told the girls to enjoy the party, then left them on their own.

Karen loved that about her mother. Annette only lingered when something went wrong.

That won't happen tonight.

Her father walked inside the room while the girls cleaned the kitchen. He stood at the outside door.

Although Sam grinned, he appeared uncomfortable. "Hello, young ladies. What time will your guests arrive, Karen?"

Karen removed cake mix boxes from the pantry. "I think

everyone should get here by seven-thirty. You don't have to build the fire for us. We can cook inside."

She glanced at him when he didn't speak.

Uncertainty highlighted the gaze that focused on her. "Are you kidding? I've looked forward to this time with you and Diane all day. Grab a jacket and come outside." Sam stepped onto the deck and closed the door behind him.

Karen turned to Diane when the girl moved forward. "Don't go outside in the cold. I'll get our coats."

She mumbled to herself as she grabbed their coats from the hall closet. It was impossible to ignore the man freezing in the cold to help her. In Karen's mind her father had laid the perfect trap for her. She admitted defeat, plodded outside, and pulled Diane along with her.

Ooh, I did this to myself. Why did I ask to grill meat when I don't know how to build a fire?

She fumed as Sam brought deck chairs into the yard. It was just like him to take advantage of her mistake. He started the fire while talking to the girls.

Sam studied his daughter with a cautious gaze. "Karen, both you and Diane take accelerated classes. I stopped by Shiatown U on the way home today. They have evening and summer curricula for honor students in high school." He glanced at Diane. "I've mentioned the program to Karen before. You girls can attend this summer at the beginning of your junior year. The credits will be applied to your college transcript."

Diane squealed but Karen damped down her excitement. This was the exact conversation he'd tried to start with her for weeks. *Now I have to submit to the interrogation.* If not, she might've appeared surly and disrespectful in front of Diane.

Karen refused to cooperate while Diane practically jumped up and down.

Her lack of response failed to dim Diane's joy. Her friend clapped her hands together.

"What do you think? I'm excited to take the courses. How about you?" She turned to Sam when Karen gazed away. "Is the program expensive?"

"Not when you consider the advantages for high school students." His gaze never left his daughter's face until he glanced at her friend. "I'm glad you're interested. I laid a pamphlet on the dining room table for you to show your parents. Now to convince my daughter. Your mother and I truly want you to consider the program. It will give you a boost when applying for scholarships."

"Why am I just hearing about the program this year? Why didn't Brenda do it?"

"We found out about the curriculum two months ago. Too late for your sister, but at least you and Jason can take advantage of the offer."

His gaze pleaded for her to say yes. To talk to him.

Dad why are you doing this to us? Why can't you let me alone? We live in the same house. Why do we have to be friends?

The question in Sam's eyes hooked her in. He wore the same hopeful expression whenever he looked at her.

Doesn't he get that I love him? I'll go crazy if I don't keep my distance from him.

"I don't know. It's sounds like a lot of hard work to me."

"This is an opportunity to glimpse the college scene before you graduate from high school. The experience factor alone will increase your confidence level."

"Please, Karen. Let's do it. We'll have loads of fun if we attend together."

"It sounds great but let me think about it first. Don't forget, I take drama lessons twice a week. I want to try out for one act plays this summer."

Sam stared at her. "Really? No one mentioned that to me. Have you asked permission from your mom?"

"Not yet. I was searching for the best time to bring it up. Please think about my acting career before you say no."

Compassion filled Sam's eyes. "Our decisions are based on what we believe is best for you. In my book academics supersede dreams. But this is a conversation the three of us will have in depth. There's ample time to fine tune the details."

Sam won a sneaky victory in the end. He tricked Karen into giving him a topic for the next discussion he hoped to have.

He's probably planning the next one-on-one while looking innocent.

Then Sam switched the topic to their college plans.

Karen almost gave a cheer once the fire gave out the perfect heat for grilling. Good thing the master fire builder didn't stay too long. The short appearance worked for Karen. She could stop giving him details about her life. He might've wormed more information from her had he stuck around longer.

She removed the roaster filled with meat from the refrigerator once inside the house.

Sam stood by the doorway to the hall. His gaze followed her movements around the kitchen.

Karen refused to look at him. "Diane, it's time to grill the meat."

The girls hesitated at the outside door instead of leaving the kitchen. Sam looked like a rejected man, but Karen lacked the will to change course.

I can't pretend you didn't hurt my mother.

He waited until Diane opened the door. "Okay, you guys, I'm out of here. Annette and I are upstairs if you need us."

Out of excuses to stay around, the whistling man joined his wife upstairs.

All in all, the Duncans projected an image of a perfect family. Yet Karen no longer believed in the fairy tale that died last spring. Had the affair been a one-time failure as her father claimed? Maybe if he'd been honest up front, she could trust his word now. Her mother did. But she was his wife and wanted to believe him.

Karen bolted the door on everything Sam.

"I've got it. Let's test out the karaoke machine while the meat grills."

Back inside the family room, her tuneless voice hit all the wrong notes. But Diane could sing, and Karen clapped the entire time she sang, happy to egg her on. It was a gift Diane should definitely pursue. There were plenty of opportunities for a person with her talent.

An hour later, the cooking was finished. The vegetable salad was in the refrigerator, and cupcakes baked in the oven. Karen dried off her hands on a paper towel and checked her watch. Six o'clock. The girls had just about completed their numerous tasks. Time to unwind before the party.

She glanced at her friend, who peered at the cupcakes through the oven glass. "I almost forgot Jason's dartboard set."

"I've always wanted to learn how to play. I'm surprised he's letting you borrow it this time."

"So is he."

Karen left her friend to check the cupcakes and bounded up the stairs. Their entire family liked to throw a round of darts. It was a game most of her friends enjoyed playing. She dashed into his bedroom and swiped the dartboard off the wall. Jason was stingy with his stuff. He would've said no if she'd even asked politely.

Back downstairs, she poked her head into the kitchen, waving the dartboard. "Let's try it out."

Diane put another batch of cupcakes into the oven, then hurried behind her. "I've waited all year to play darts."

In the family room, Karen discovered something else about her friend. Diane was a natural at throwing darts. She beat Karen, who usually bested everyone she played, except her brother.

Finished playing, the girls went back to the kitchen. Diane grabbed a towel from the rack and headed straight to the oven.

Karen slouched against the counter. She felt terrible about taking the dartboard. She would've threatened Jason had he entered her bedroom without permission. Jokes with Diane didn't make her feel any better. She called him and received the first shock of the night. Jason said yes without setting conditions. He usually made her pay a hefty price to borrow his things. The laughter in the background proved he was having fun. No wonder he swiftly agreed. Jason wanted to get back to the noise.

Then Brenda dropped into the kitchen for a snack break. Karen's friends loved her older sister. Brenda ignored the girls in the group who weren't invited to the pajama party. But she regularly talked to Karen's other friends. This time, her sister chatted awhile but didn't stay long. She'd sworn off all communication until the term paper was finished. Even her boyfriend had been told not to call, text, or drop by for a visit. Brenda claimed she couldn't study with people around.

After her sister left, Karen carried four bowls filled with snacks into the family room. She placed her load on the only table left. She walked into the hall, chewing on a potato chip. Then headlights flashed through the foyer window. Karen saw three girls step out of the car parked in the driveway. She rushed forward and switched on the intercom attached to the wall. Guilt struck her while she peeked outside. Eavesdropping was wrong. Her mother would be angry if she caught her at it. The intercom had been installed for another purpose. She almost turned it off, but then the conversation began.

Oh well. Too late to tune out now. I might as well listen.

Karen watched the girls lug their sleepover gear to the steps. For once, their nonstop chatter had been abandoned. But having their hands filled with stuff failed to explain their subdued behavior. Unless …

Joann broke the silence after she reached the steps. The five-six, raven-haired, blue-eyed beauty towered over the other girls. "I don't see Angela's or Linda's cars. Good. I'm glad we're the first ones here."

"Too bad, we're not. Diane Meredith went home with Karen after school today," said Lisa.

Her pouty speech concerned Karen. She pressed her forehead onto the glass as she remembered her promise to Diane. Lisa was still upset about seeing Diane and Karen walking home together after school. She acted awful whenever she became angry.

I'm holding you to your promise. You better be nice to Diane. If you renege … well, I'll think of something.

"*Diane Meredith*," Kathy mocked in a singsong voice. "Why do you always use her entire name?"

The shortest girl in the group was the spunkiest person Karen knew. Big or small, Kathy challenged everyone she met.

Joann trudged up the steps. "Stop finding fault. We're not even inside the house yet."

Karen moved to the door. She reached for the lock but lowered her hand once the talking resumed. She went back to the window.

"I was speaking to Lisa, not you." Kathy jerked her head toward Joann before she faced Lisa. "It's a serious question, so answer it."

Karen peeked around the curtain but she hid when Joann looked straight at her.

Kathy won't give up. She has spent some of her happiest moments harassing Lisa.

Lisa turned her back to Kathy when her sleeping bag slipped. She inched the bundle back into her arms with her knee. "Stop being pushy. They left school after their silly little reporters' meeting. It seems that Karen forgot to tell me Diane was going home with her after school. I saw them lug Diane's stuff down the street before I met you."

Joann nodded while she started toward the door.

Kathy blocked Lisa's way. "Silly little reporters' meeting, huh? You're jealous because you can't write a complete sentence."

Joann spun around and almost toppled over. "Look, Lisa forgot you're on the newspaper staff, too, okay? People know you for your cheers, not your stories."

"They're silly. It's more important to write articles than lead cheers. Anybody can flaunt themselves in public. Only a few of us can truly write."

Karen played with the curtain. Should she let the girls stay for the party or send them back home?

Oh, my goodness. Until recently, I acted horrible too, arguing just to argue. Now, I try not to do it. Only, it's hard to be nice to people who don't deserve it.

Especially when the things she shouldn't say were true.

Even though it was cold outside, her friends kept talking. On the porch, Karen could clearly see their faces in the light.

Lisa grinned at Joann then snickered in Kathy's face. "So, the three of you enjoy getting writer's cramp? Well, good for you. Stop putting down cheerleaders. Next you'll claim there's nothing to twirling flags."

Kathy almost choked on her laughter. "You said it, color guard."

"You wouldn't blow off our skill if you had to keep in step with a mediocre band," Joann said.

Kathy dropped her sleeping bag to swat the finger Lisa wagged in her face. "Stop trashing the Tigers. I guess you color guards need to practice more. News flash! Our band took second place in a statewide competition."

Lisa sidestepped Kathy and reached the door. "Just goes to show how terrible the other bands sounded."

"Both of you sound silly trashing our newspaper and band. Lisa says Diane's full name because she's jealous. It's cold out here. Don't hold your finger over the doorbell; ring it."

"Jo, just let Karen know that Kathy started fussing first." Lisa rang the doorbell after she stuck out her tongue at Kathy.

Chapter Five

Karen quickly opened the door, pulled a startled Lisa inside the house, then shivered when Lisa rubbed her cold face on Karen's cheek.

She stepped away and rubbed her hands over her face.

"Yeah, it's cold outside. What took you so long to open the door?"

"You just rang the doorbell, Lisa. I was listening on the intercom. I'm surprised you stood outside talking so long. It's freezing."

Kathy breezed past the girls huddled in the foyer. She dropped her gear at their feet. "Then why did you leave us in the cold instead of opening the door? I guess you heard Lisa get upset at a simple question. She always uses Diane's full name."

Karen backed up a few steps then pointed toward the back of the house. "Diane's in the kitchen frosting cupcakes. She made dozens of them for us to eat."

"So what?" asked Lisa. "I'm fed up with Kathy claiming I'm jealous of her."

Kathy mouthed the word "sorry" to Karen, and then she spoke to Lisa in a lower voice. "Then call her Diane like a normal person. Everyone else does. Why not you?"

"Wait," said Lisa, hanging her coat inside the hall closet. "I'm jealous because I say her full name? What world do you live in?"

Oh, boy. They still don't get it. Time to take charge.

"Diane's waiting for us in the kitchen, and ... we're serving—"

"Why do you keep saying she's in the kitchen? Have I said anything wrong? Tell Kathy to stop annoying me before I unload on *her.*"

Kathy burst into laughter. "Let me have it, Lisa. *I* fight back."

No one loved verbal arguments more than Kathy. She was the official battle wager among her friends. Karen looked at Joann for help, but she'd distanced herself from the friction—although Joann probably sought ways to side with Lisa.

What can I say that Lisa will agree to? Anything to keep her quiet.

"I have a change of plans. Put everything against the wall. You can grab stuff as you need it. We'll eat in the family room instead of the kitchen. I'll get Diane." She walked away, then stopped in her tracks, and spun around. "Don't forget to turn off your cell phones. Outside communication is banned tonight. Remind your folks to call the house phone number if they want you."

On her way to the kitchen Karen glimpsed Diane as she sat inside the family room.

Oh no. She overheard what Lisa said. Diane wouldn't have heard us talking had she stayed in the kitchen. Oh, Lisa. I promised Diane that you would behave yourself tonight.

Karen slipped inside the room and knelt beside her on the floor. She hesitated when tears formed in Diane's eyes. Diane turned away, brushing teardrops off her cheeks.

"It'll get better. No one said anything bad about you."

Disbelief entered Diane's eyes. "I guess not. You warned them enough times that I was in the kitchen and might hear every word they said."

At that moment, Kathy pranced into the room. She sat across

from the girls, while her gaze swept the space. Finally, she tilted her head to the side. A grin lit up her face. "Hi, Diane. I couldn't wait to get here. We're going to have fun tonight."

"You think so? Why? I don't see any happy people. I didn't hear any happy talk, either. I'm sick of Lisa picking on me. She didn't say more because Karen said that I could hear her."

Kathy twirled a strand of hair around her fingers. "You know that isn't true. Your overhearing what she says doesn't bother Lisa at all. She'll speak her mind if that's what she wants to do." Kathy tried again when Diane failed to reply. "Forget it. Blame me. She's upset with me for hassling her about you. I stuck up for you before we came inside."

"Don't expect a thank you. I don't want, or need, your help. Since she's your frenemy, you can explain why she always says *Diane Meredith.*"

Joann and Lisa walked into the room. They stood together in the middle of the floor until Lisa set her purse in a corner.

"Don't badger Kathy. Ask me."

Diane waited until Lisa moved closer. She rose to her knees. Her body locked into position. "What? Do I need to repeat the question for you? That figures. Why do you call me Diane Meredith?"

Surprised at the outburst, Karen remained silent. She observed the confrontation. Only Kathy appeared willing to let the feud blow over. Karen quickly decided not to intervene for now. She thought it was best to wait and see what happened.

Humor lit Lisa's face until tension shook Diane's body.

Karen knew the exact moment Lisa yielded. That was the friend she loved. The one who protected the underdog instead of annoying them to death.

"Diane Meredith flows from the tongue," Lisa said in a soft voice.

When Kathy's eyes narrowed, Karen rushed into speech. "There's food in the kitchen if anyone's hungry. Diane and I did us proud. Check it out."

Karen mouthed the words, "I beat you before you nailed Lisa," to Kathy.

Kathy winked at her. "This time," she mouthed back.

Lisa smirked at the girls' silent communication. "We ate tacos after school, although *Kathy* will probably eat again. She's always hungry."

Kathy dashed across the floor but stopped in the doorway. "So, Lisa Douglas is an expert on my eating habits. Imagine that. I *will* eat a little to save you from being a liar." She smiled at Diane who rocked back and forth. "I'll check out your cupcakes. I bet they're delicious."

Silence abounded after Kathy left the room. Sometimes quiet is soothing, but not today. Karen sensed the storm about to break over the evening. She breathed into her hand. How do I get the party on track? What can we discuss that won't make anyone angry? What topic is safe to talk about? Deep in thought, she noticed Joann toss a CD to Lisa, who read the cover, then tossed it back.

Joann obviously lost steam when Lisa failed to knock Karen's music choice, but she confronted Karen anyway. She waved the CD in her hand. "I don't see anyone I want to listen to in this case. Who are these people?"

Here we go, and Joann just got here. She'd better lay off me tonight. I'm not in the mood for her nonsense. Karen sighed, thinking of what to say. *Be nice. I invited her. It's way too early to send her home. I'll give Joann more rope until she hangs herself then boot her out.*

The threat of asking Joann to leave pleased Karen, but she knew she would never do it. Why risk her mother's wrath unnecessarily? She cleared her throat to keep the annoyance out of her voice. "Contemporary gospel singers I listen to. Why do you ask?"

"You really expect us to play these CDs all night? Groups we never heard of?"

"Only if you want to listen to music. If not, we can talk, play games, or watch movies. Come on, we always have fun at sleepovers."

Joann shoved the CD case inside the cabinet. "Remember the 'make your guest happy' rule?"

"No, and neither do you. I listen to Christian music. I gave away my other collection during the summer."

"Yeah, to Lisa and that girl at school, as if you didn't know anyone else. You gave someone my favorite artist."

Joann had a long memory about situations that meant nothing. She could, and did, buy whatever she wanted to have. Besides, Lisa had asked for those CDs, and Karen threw in a few for a girl in her social studies class because she couldn't afford to buy her own. Why whine about something she'd probably forgotten about until that moment? She sent a silent appeal to Lisa, but Diane spoke up first.

"Give us a break, Joann. My goodness, this is a one-nighter. You're not moving in. Don't you ever quit?"

Karen released the breath she held slowly. This was the second time Diane had failed to offer a peaceful solution. She felt like slapping each girl. They were turning her sleepover into a warzone.

"I haven't heard any of those CDs," said Lisa, "but I'm willing to listen to one." She removed a purple barrette from her pocket, and bunched her curls into a ponytail. Hazel eyes glowed in her toffee-colored face. "For now, I'm waiting for Linda to come."

Karen's chin dropped to her chest. She wanted to crawl into

her bed and go to sleep. Too bad she couldn't listen in on Evette's and Linda's conversation. Will they be in a better mood than this bunch?

* * *

Linda Ferguson parked her car in front of Karen's house. This was the first time she'd been invited to visit since seventh grade. Her elementary school years were spent romping throughout the place. The landscape still provided the perfect picture. Manicured lawn and trimmed shrubbery displayed the same curb appeal. She loved that lights shone brightly on the porch and from the windows. The homey scene brought back happy memories. It helped her think that coming to the party might be a good thing.

Linda was of two minds about being here. She was happy to learn what this pajama party was all about, yet sad to turn down a date with a boy she'd been interested in since school started. But she'd already promised to bring Evette before he called this evening. She was stuck with her previous choice. Oh well, she'd chosen. With luck, it would be the correct decision. If not, Linda wouldn't make it through the night.

Distracted, she took a backpack from inside her car trunk and handed it to Evette. She watched as Evette struggled to hook it onto her shoulders. Linda reached back inside the trunk and removed three blankets and a pillow. She plopped the bundle onto Evette's arms, turned around in slow motion, and slammed the trunk. After Linda retrieved her own stuff from the backseat, she kicked the door shut with her foot.

It all seemed like wasted energy to Linda because she halfway expected to have a miserable time. Perhaps she should've accepted the date and gone to the basketball game. But Linda showed up because she wanted this party to work. She came over this evening for an opportunity to reconnect with Karen.

As they moved toward the porch, she eyed the car parked in the Duncans' driveway. Darn it. Joann and crew had beat them here, even though Linda had left home early enough to get here first. Her gaze darted to the girl who caused their late arrival. Linda had twiddled her thumbs while Evette finished up her housework.

Instead of being packed and ready to go, Evette washed dishes and then tidied up the house in general. She had five younger brothers and sisters to help clean up after. One child crawled around on the floor in diapers, while the next one up, a toddler, could barely walk. They lived in a very small house for a large family. No more than three bedrooms, from the look of it. The tiny living room was overrun with people. The spotless house smelled of fresh fruit.

Although the children obeyed Evette's directions when given, Evette had Linda's sympathy. Being the oldest daughter of three girls, Linda understood the responsibilities placed on the eldest sibling. She usually complained about what she had to do, but she realized that her chores were nothing in comparison to Evette's.

Oh well, Joann and her crowd had beat them here. There wasn't a way to swap that reality with her wishes. She looked back at Evette, who treaded up the driveway. She moved slowly, as if she hated to take each step. Why would she put herself through unnecessary misery? Evette should've said no if she didn't want to come.

Chapter Six

Linda nodded toward the car she'd eyed a few minutes earlier. "That little black job belongs to Joann. A birthday gift from her parents for the big one six."

Evette slowed her steps even more, inspecting the vehicle when they reached it. She moved away from the car. "Is she rich?"

"Her folks are loaded. They own several fast-food restaurants across the state."

"I'm surprised. No one would think Joann had a dime by the way she dresses."

"Shabby chic. Joann would look good wearing a sack. She splurges when she shops. Last Saturday, she paid fifty-five dollars for an ugly key chain. She waved it underneath my nose Monday."

"Now why doesn't that surprise me?" Evette squinted her eyes at Karen's house. "I can't imagine why I was invited, or why I agreed to come. Do you think everyone will act okay tonight? Think I'll fit in?"

In a hurry to get out of the cold, Linda kept walking. "Have fun? Yes. Karen will have lots of things for us to do. I attended all her pajama parties when we were younger. You'll be fine tonight. But don't expect that any of them grew up since they left school this afternoon."

"Good point. At least Sandy is coming. I really like her. Why does she run around with that crowd?"

"She doesn't. Sandy has her own set of friends. Those girls she eats lunch with have been her buddies since elementary school."

"I eat lunch at a different time than Sandy. I see her hanging out with Karen's gang in the hall, so I thought they were friends." She placed her blankets and pillow on a porch chair.

Linda set down her load to ring the doorbell. Then she dropped her hand before she pushed the button.

"Sandy walks with Karen, who hangs out with the gang. They're cousins."

"I didn't know that. At first, Karen seemed snooty when I met her. She's cool. But her friends act weird. Today they were complaining because she only invited three of them tonight. Why did she include you and me but leave them out? Have they always been buddies?"

"Of the girls invited, four of us started kindergarten together. Angela was in second grade. Joann, Kathy, and Diane came to Jefferson Middle in sixth grade. The rest of the group came in seventh grade. Why are you frowning?"

"It's because you all grew up together but barely talk to each other. I've only seen Diane with Karen. Their group is hard to figure out. I used to think they hated each other until I saw them away from school. I've spotted them around town, but Karen is never with them."

Linda's eyes narrowed. "You're right. Away from school, I've only seen her with the three girls coming tonight. Humph, I hadn't thought about that before. Anyway, I suppose it's complicated to newbies, and maybe to me now that I reconsider the Karen angle."

"They're too dramatic and argue all the time."

Linda stretched her hand toward the doorbell, but Evette grabbed her arm.

Linda yanked her arm away from her grip. "I'm freezing! I've given you loads of information. Let's go inside."

"Fill me in. I should've asked you in the car on the way over. Just give me a quick rundown so I can know what to expect tonight. Maybe they act more strange than weird."

Linda shook her head. "Is there a difference? You know this is ridiculous. Karen *is* nicer, *this year.* She and Diane became friends in ninth grade. But Lisa and Karen have been best friends since kindergarten. So Lisa is jealous of Karen and Diane's relationship."

Linda hated to speak about people who weren't there, but she went right on. What else could she do? Evette seemed determined to make her freeze to death. Or, at the very least, catch pneumonia. "It's like this: Diane is only friends with Karen. Diane isn't part of their group. Karen likes her. Kathy has tried to make Joann *her* best friend since sixth grade, but Joann prefers palling around with Lisa."

"Lisa! Why? The girl acts horrible most of the time. She isn't mean like their other friends but she's close enough."

Linda stifled her laughter. It was too cold to gossip *and* have fun. "Joann likes Lisa a lot. She thinks she and Lisa have more in common than Lisa and Karen, or Kathy and herself for that matter."

"She's right on track about that. Joann and Lisa deserve each other."

Linda rang the doorbell. "You said that, not me. I've given you enough information. Now you need to form your own opinion."

"It's too late to back out now. I won't ask you to take me home. I'm just ... feeling a little nervous about going inside. Like I'm starring in a movie without a script. What role do we play?"

"That's it! A scene in Karen's homemade movie and we're

winging it. Too bad I don't have a clue to the end game. But relax. Karen's house is safe ground. We'll be okay."

A bright smile lit Linda's face when a girl peeked at them through a side window. "It's my favorite person. This is going to be a fun night. Count on it."

Her weariness vanished once she peeped inside the foyer. Even though the house had a different layout than the last time she had visited, the familiar parts brought comfort. Somehow, she felt better seeing Brenda instead of her sister. The older girl always treated Linda like a friend. But the younger one had forgotten about her old-school pal. That was the main reason she decided to join the party. Why had Karen invited Linda to come over to her house tonight? Karen always stopped to talk whenever they passed by each other in the hall at school. But she hadn't asked Linda to get together after school until this sleepover.

She stepped into the house. "Hi, Brenda, this is Evette Nichols. Her family moved to Shiatown last summer." She moved aside and allowed Evette to enter the foyer before she continued the introduction. "Evette, Brenda is the coolest older sister I know. She's a freshman at Shiatown U and my role model. I'm mirroring myself after her. My younger sisters deserve better than what they get from me."

Brenda smiled at both girls while holding onto the door handle. "Aw, shucks, don't believe her. Linda is a wonderful big sister."

Linda jumped when she heard a thump against the wall from the other side. The noise was quickly followed by shrieks, laughter, and overexcited voices that talked at once. Another crash sounded, as if something had exploded, followed by more objects hitting the wall.

Evette's eyebrows arched just below her hairline. She shivered on her feet.

"I see they started the games without us," said Linda. "I'm surprised your mom is still upstairs. Has it been this way all night?"

"Yes, the noise level continues to climb. They can't hear the doorbell ring over that racket. Good thing I took a snack break."

Brenda locked the door then switched her gaze to the other girl. "Hi, Evette. Karen told me you were coming tonight. I work with the middle schoolers at church on Wednesdays. Your younger sister is in my starburst class. I saw you pick her up one night."

Evette smiled for the first time since she got into Linda's car. "Church. I knew I'd seen you somewhere. But I've never seen Karen there. Not even on Sundays."

"On Sundays she sits in the balcony, and she takes drama lessons in the learning center on Wednesdays."

Brenda headed toward the stairs but turned around before she reached them.

"Say hi the next time you pick up your sister. Stack your things in the corner by the closet, then head to the family room. Linda knows the way." She grinned as she lingered on the bottom step. "Feel free to add to the noise decibel as much as you like. Everyone else has."

Linda watched Brenda sprint up the steps before she headed down the hallway. The layout in the house seemed awkward to her. Things were recognizable and unknown at the same time. A major renovation had overhauled the space.

The thump sounded again, but it seemed farther away this time. Only one game could create such a racket. It happened to be her favorite game to play.

She strolled into the family room. Like a shadow, Evette followed close behind her.

The other girls failed to see them at the door.

Chapter Seven

Karen glanced up and spotted Linda and Evette as they entered the room. Still seated, she studied the girls, amazed at the ill-at-ease Evette. She looked like she was hoping to blend in with the woodwork.

Loosen up. You're going to be happy you joined us.

Karen decided to greet them without getting up. "Hi, guys. We were waiting for you two to get here. Join the fun. I heard this was someone's favorite game. I bought it over the weekend. We're still learning how to play."

Linda set her purse against the wall, and motioned to Evette to do the same. "From the commotion, I knew you were playing *The Domino Effect*. Who fell against the wall? What exploded?" She pointed across the room. "Are you imitating a crying monkey?"

Diane stopped in mid-action. "Crying monkey! No, I'm a horse whisperer." She wiggled her fingers at Linda then grinned at the other girl. "Hi, Evette. I've been waiting for you two to get here."

"Me too," said Lisa. She sauntered toward the girls.

Linda met her halfway. They hugged, then chatted in the middle of the room.

Evette resembled a lost child once Linda left her side. Her deflated shoulders slumped even more when the girls continued to talk.

Lisa peered around Linda and stared into the hallway. She frowned, gazed from Linda to Evette, then stared into the hall again.

"Where's the sleeping bag I've told everyone about? It's too cute."

Linda crossed to the other girls and plunked down on the floor. "We brought blankets and left our stuff by the front hall closet."

She nudged Kathy with her hip. "Scoot over."

"Perfect," said Karen. "We'll bring the sleep gear in later. Did you remember to turn off your cell phones?"

Linda nodded, but Evette said she didn't own one to turn off.

"I really want one of those sleeping bags, just like the picture you showed me," Lisa said. "Joann and I tried to find one like it, but Callahan's had sold out. Why didn't you bring ..." she paused, and faced Evette. She placed two fingers across her lips. "Oh. No cell phone. Do you own a sleeping bag?"

Red blotches appeared on Evette's cheeks. She parted her lips then studied her shoes. She took a deep breath. "Karen, thanks for inviting me."

"Talk to me," said Lisa. "I want to help. Had I known, I would've brought my little sister's sleeping bag."

Skepticism replaced the dismay plastered on Evette's face. "I think many things about you, but being thoughtful isn't one of them."

Karen popped up off the floor in a hurry. She crossed the room and wedged herself between the girls as they faced each other.

She moved her friend aside. "Only her closest friends realize how kind Lisa is. It's after seven. Look in the kitchen if you're hungry. I loaded the counter with food."

If Lisa stays silent we're home free. Why is everyone just staring? Kathy, help me out.

"That was an insult. Are you accusing me of something?" Lisa asked.

Evette's eyes widened. She took a step backward.

"Don't back down now. I'll respect you more if you say it out loud."

Evette's expression flashed regret, but there wasn't a way to retract the hasty words she'd spoken. Her lower lip trembled as if she might burst into tears at any moment. "Karen, did you ever find out—" She closed her eyes when Lisa interrupted.

"No, missy, it isn't that easy. If you disrespect me when I'm being nice, you're going to deal with me when I'm not."

Karen weighed her options as she grabbed Evette's hand. She didn't see an easy way out. "Lisa, I'm—"

"Stay out of it! What would my ulterior motive be in telling Evette I would've brought her a sleeping bag?"

"Your *little sister's* sleeping bag. Really? You implied Linda brought a blanket because of me."

Lisa laughed. "She did, so admit it. You want to fight with me about a sleeping bag? Get over yourself."

"Who cares about who brought whatever?" Joann said. "Change the subject. Talk about something else."

"No. The girl accused me of having ulterior motives."

"Ulterior ..." said Kathy. "Lisa's building up her vocabulary. Get it, girl."

"You're hilarious. Evette's upset because she came to a sleepover without a sleeping bag. It's *her* attitude problem. I was being thoughtful."

Evette sniffled and ran a finger across her nose. "There's nothing wrong with my attitude. It was fine before I got here. I don't understand why Karen invited me. I came to get to know you all better. To enjoy myself and have fun." Her hands rubbed her upper arms. "Whether I bring a blanket or a sleeping bag shouldn't be an issue."

Red streaks rose on Evette's neck, and Karen's heart turned over.

"It isn't an issue. The offer of the sleeping bag was real and not intended as an insult. Lisa lives around the corner. She would've gone home and brought it back. Ask Linda, if you don't believe me. If you're hungry, the food is in the kitchen. There are towels in the bathroom linen closest. I'll show you the way."

"That's okay I'm hungry too. I'll show her," Linda said.

Karen nodded. "Diane's cupcakes are scrumptious. I ate two. Kathy said the food tastes delicious. Eat up."

Linda hooked her arm through Evette's, propelling the girl toward the door. Diane, who stood across the room, pushed away the game they were playing. She ran up behind the girls, wrapped her arms around Linda's neck, and left the room with them.

Karen felt sucker-punched. She closed her eyes to critique the situation. Lisa's delivery was off. She'd sounded snotty, but that fact didn't explain why Evette jumped to the wrong conclusion. From the look on Lisa's face, she was finally serious about being misunderstood.

I'm tired of taking the lead with people who refuse to cooperate with me.

"What just happened? I didn't see that one coming."

"Me neither." Kathy frowned and turned to Lisa. "Well, that was tactless, even for you."

"Pick the right side! The girl jumped *me*. She blew up over a sleeping bag."

"Okay, the offer was genuine, but the way you phrased it sounded mean. You have this superior air that ... Lisa, you rub people the wrong way."

"Don't blame me for your inferiority complex. Get real or get lost. Whatever—you decide."

Kathy massaged her temples. "Karen, Lisa isn't on the same page with us. Are you sure God told you to have this pajama party?"

"God?!" said Lisa and Joann together.

Karen shrugged. "Maybe I missed what God wanted me to do. I guess it's possible. I've been wrong before. Still, I stand by my belief that this pajama party is a good thing. If we do it right."

"Stop talking in code and explain why you shared a secret with Kathy without telling me," said Lisa.

Sympathy highlighted Kathy's face as she smiled at Karen. "Get serious," said Kathy. "We were talking about God. Don't change the subject. Apologize to Evette. She isn't used to you."

"Forget that. She attacked me after I chose to be friendly."

Kathy sighed as she placed her palm on her forehead. "Does that matter at this point? Just apologize to her. Please. See? I asked *nicely.*"

"Why does it always come to me to back down first? What if she rejects my apology after I put myself out there? Then what? Apologize again?"

"If she dismisses you, it's her problem. You go first. It'll be a *first.*"

Karen winked at Kathy. *Sweet.*

Lisa tilted her head to the side. She pretended to be deep in thought. She yawned, and covered her mouth with her hand, coughed, and squeezed her lips together. By the time she rubbed her chin with her forefinger and thumb, Karen wanted to throttle her. It seemed like the girl took hours to reach a decision.

I hope Lisa's attitude isn't a sign about the rest of the night.

"Joann, should I apologize to that—"

"We agreed you would be nice to Diane tonight," Karen said.

"That promise included Evette and everyone else who comes. Your word is becoming meaningless." She wanted to press Lisa into agreeing before Joann disrupted the plan.

"Okay. I remember. This is my good-girl night. What would you do in my place, Jo?"

Karen covered her face with her hands. "Wrong question. Wrong person." She removed her hands and stared at Lisa. "Get serious. *Please.* Now, I asked *nicely*, too. Two against one. We're not counting Joann."

Joann threw a popcorn kernel at Karen before she answered. "Apologize and get it over with," she said to Lisa. "Trust me, it's the lesser of two evils. In a way, Evette was justified for getting upset. She doesn't know us."

Lisa parted her lips then clamped them shut. "Okay, I'll tell her I'm sorry."

"No!" said Kathy. "She may believe you. The word sorry has more than one meaning. You know that."

Karen held up both hands. "I'm calling a truce because it's a done deal. Lisa will apologize and that's it." She checked her watch and smiled. "Sandy and Angela should get here in twenty minutes. That should calm us down some. Neither of them have a problem with anyone here."

A cell phone chimed.

Karen stared at the guilty-faced culprit. "Turn it off, Joann. Does anyone else still have their cell phone on?"

Kathy and Lisa said, "No." But Joann grinned at the screen then laid the cell phone beside her.

"Sorry, I thought it was on vibrate. Cal just checked in. He claims he's home for the night. Liar. Just like the other two that texted before him. Now they can all go out while they pretend to be at home for the night."

"You have too many boys to keep up with," said Kathy. "Next

time, find out where they're going beforehand. I know Joey is at the movies with friends. After that, he'll head to Burger Barn. Unlike me, the ten-thirty wonder, he has a midnight curfew on weekends."

"Well, your parents let him visit once he brings you home. The guys I date don't think like Joey. They'll tell me where they're going then change their minds and go someplace else."

"What difference does that make? You don't care where they go or who they go with. Would it bother you if they slipped out with another girl?"

"Only because it meant they lied to me. But other than that, it wouldn't. So let's talk about you and Joey. I sense commitment in the air. That comment you made sounds like you're keeping tabs on his whereabouts. Are you all in?"

"As in as I care to be. I like our relationship the way it is. So does Joey." Kathy turned to Karen. "Okay, you've been sixteen for thirty days. Ready to start dating?"

"Not so much, now. I don't like the boys who asks me out."

"Can't muster up enthusiasm for the wide receiver, the center guard, or the class president?" asked Joann. "Wish I had your problems."

"No, you don't. Then you'll juggle six boys instead of three."

The sound of voices in the hallway announced Diane, Linda, and Evette's arrival from the kitchen. All three faces wore smiles when they walked in. It seemed that the unplanned separation had had a good effect.

Karen's spirit soared until Lisa rose to meet the girls at the door.

Linda walked up to her and offered chips from the bowl she carried.

The light in Lisa's eyes gleamed with either mischief or regret, but her body language depicted a shy nature.

"Evette," she said, and shuffled closer. She carefully chose each word she spoke. "I'm sorry. Really sorry."

Evette nodded then looked confused when Linda and Diane burst into laughter.

Karen could hardly believe that both girls ridiculed Lisa as Lisa tried to start over with Evette. Karen had begged her to make it right. Now Linda and Diane threw the effort back into Lisa's face. No one deserved to be mocked, her best friend included. Karen laid her head on Lisa's shoulder. A tremor surged through the embarrassed girl's body.

She's hurt by the same treatment she's given to others. I would be too.

Kathy glared at Linda and Diane. "Hmm, giggles. That means you both know the word 'sorry' has more than one meaning. Glad you're literate. But that doesn't excuse the low blow you gave to Lisa. Too bad. I expected more maturity from both of you."

Joann scowled at both girls. "First me and now Lisa. You're unusually feisty, Diane." She eyed Evette. "I see that you came with Linda. I dislike two-faced people. How about you?"

"Oh really. I can either forget that remark or punch you." Linda pointed her finger at Kathy. "You too. This time, I choose to forget." She shifted toward Lisa. "Sorry. Or should I say, I apologize. Either way, I really mean it. Friends for life?"

Chapter Eight

Lisa did a shorter version of her thinking-about-it routine. "Well, I guess so. At least until I wake up in the morning. My promise to Karen surpasses my feelings about you and Diane. I stick by my friends." She rubbed her cheek against Karen's hair. "See, I keep my word, friend. Trust me." Her eyes sparkled as she smiled.

Diane rushed into speech. "So do I. Forgive me for laughing. That comment wasn't even funny."

Lisa frowned. "Question. Why are you apologizing to Karen and not to me?"

"I'm not apologizing to just Karen, but to everyone here. I was wrong to laugh."

"Nah, I think you timed everything perfect. Go on, show Karen that what I've always known about you is true."

Karen narrowed her eyes. "Lisa, lighten up. Diane apologized."

"So laughing in someone's face is okay if they apologize?"

"Get with the program," Kathy said. "People apologize when they want to turn the page. Reasonable people let them do it."

Diane peered at Lisa. "You've lost me. What can you tell my friend that she doesn't already know?"

"What you're hiding, perhaps?"

"If I'm hiding anything it's in your imagination."

"Cute," said Lisa. "Karen likes you too much to pay attention to your barbs. The night is young. You'll mess up again before it ends."

Diane walked out of the room without responding to Lisa's taunt. When Evette followed behind her, Karen decided not to go. Had a friendship begun during their time in the kitchen? If so, this was the first answer to Karen's get-together prayers. If she interfered it might stop the relationship before it developed further.

Besides, her thoughts were scattered all over the place. Instead of hosting her party, she wanted to hide out in her bedroom, and replay the latest confrontation. Somehow, everyone's roles had been reversed. It turned her world upside down. Except for Evette, these were the girls she'd grown up with and known practically all her life. But now she felt like she didn't know them at all.

Even though Karen had witnessed miracles arise from her family problems, when good sprang out of heartbreak, it still boggled her mind. All the needless conflicts that had played out in the family room reminded her of just that. Pointless trouble. So far, everything had been a muddled mess.

Yet, within fifteen minutes, the girls came back and quietly sat together. They eyed the group. Still upset, Diane's quivering lips curved into a lopsided smile. Only the pink eyes and red-tipped nose proved she'd had a crying spell.

Noticeably happy, Evette's body wiggled like someone who danced on cloud nine. The grin remained on her lips long after she sat down.

To break the ice, Kathy produced a cloth pouch that held a small ball and ten jacks. Her granny had taught her how to play the game before Kathy started kindergarten. Karen loved to play the old-fashioned game. The girls who had never played before absorbed themselves in learning the rules. Hand-eye coordination was required to play well. The beginners caught on fast and improved their skills.

Amazed by the harmony inside the room, Karen studied everyone while they played. They all joked and gabbed like old buddies. Everyone was peaceful now, but who knew what nonsense might set them off again.

By tomorrow, will I even care about how this sleepover ends? If not, won't that make me as wishy-washy as my friends?

Then Lisa spoke to Karen in a stage whisper loud enough for everyone to hear. "Don't you hate it when someone says they're sensitive then proves themselves to be anything but? I offend others *way* too much to make that claim. Still, I find it hilarious that those same people—the ones with the paper-thin skins—expect to stand in front of a moving train and not get splattered. How could they think that?"

Kathy whispered into Karen's ear, "You knew it was coming. That situation is hardly over."

"No," said Karen as she whispered back, "I forgot she won't let things go."

Then Kathy and Karen stared at Lisa who gazed back at them and tried to keep from laughing.

After Lisa's offhand remark, the strife morphed into a reluctant acceptance of the facts. Unless someone left early, they were stuck with each other until morning. Apparently, speaking truthfully cleared the air of false hopes. Perhaps that they knew each other's true intentions erased the intimidation factor.

Whatever the cause, they suddenly got along, and then the real fun began. Each girl opted to enjoy herself instead of fighting with one another. Even though a truce of sorts had been called, the occasional hostile look continued to surface. Beyond that, everyone finally settled down to have a good time.

First they took turns at the karaoke machine. Diane was the

only person who could truly sing, although Evette could do more than hold a note. An eager Kathy almost convinced both girls to take voice lessons at the community center. She herself took weekly tennis lessons there during the fall and winter seasons. Then she competed in matches during the spring and summer months.

Just as Karen put aside the microphone, Annette dropped in to say hello to the newest arrivals and asked about their families. Good thing she hadn't come downstairs earlier while the claws showed. Since the girls behaved themselves, Karen welcomed the visit. She liked to see her mom mingle with her friends. It proved that her mother cared about everything that involved her daughter. Her acknowledgment of Karen's friends was the right thing to do *if* she didn't stay too long. Karen was happy as long as Annette left when Karen wanted her to leave.

Her mom stole the show. She smiled while Evette explained why Mrs. Nichols allowed Evette to come over without a phone call. "My mom and dad ate dinner with you and your husband at the civic meeting last month. They still rave about the fantastic time they had talking to you."

Karen frowned when Annette looked her way with an expression that clearly read, "See, not everyone has a bad impression of your father."

Her mother remained long enough to remind the girls that she was in the house. After that, she headed to the door. "You girls enjoy yourselves. My husband rented several movies for the two of us to watch tonight. Take the stairs and turn left on the landing if you need me for any reason. We're behind the double doors at the end of the hall."

Joann walked out of the room behind Annette when she left, but she came back quickly with an overnight case. She opened it up and unpacked her cosmetics and nail polish kit. Then she pulled out a few items and offered to play a makeup artist. Each girl eagerly accepted the offer. Joann always looked makeup-free even though she'd worn the stuff since seventh grade.

Everyone gathered around her on the floor to observe her technique while she made over Lisa. They all oohed and aahed as Lisa blossomed into an even prettier version of herself.

The offer proved to be a big hit. Each girl wanted to receive their makeover next. Joann used a soft touch. The outcome revealed a definite talent as she highlighted everyone's best features. Since Lisa's makeover was finished, she polished the other girls' fingernails.

Karen noticed headlights shine through the drapes while she waited her turn.

"I'll be right back," she said. Not making eye contact with anyone, she scurried out the door.

Karen grabbed her coat from the hall closet and zipped it up while she navigated through the dark garage. She braced for the cruel wind, slipped outside the side door, and darted around the house. Then she beckoned the two girls who walked across the driveway. "Come in through the garage. You're late, but strangely right on time."

Karen hurriedly retraced her steps and switched on a light inside the garage. She wrapped her arms around her body in an attempt to thaw out.

Angela closed the garage door behind her. Concern highlighted her features. "How can we be both? Do we need to know something before we go in?"

"Yes ..." Karen paused to watch Sandy blow a bubble that was larger than her face. "Stop distracting me. Now I forgot what I wanted to say."

Sandy sucked the bubble into her mouth. "Sounds like we're too late to stop whatever happened, but we're in time to stop it before it happens again." She threw her gum into a trash can. "Did I get that right?" She spoke before Karen answered. "Lisa and Kathy, or Lisa and Diane?"

"Well, you know how Lisa and Diane react to each other, but Lisa's argument with Evette surprised me. I know," she said when Sandy did a double take. "The entire scene was unbelievable to watch. There's more to Evette than we suspected."

Angela raised her eyebrows. "Did Evette and Lisa argue about something specific? What set it off?"

"I told you she was a paradox."

Karen looked at her as if that comment answered the question.

"Yeah, I had to look up the word to refresh my memory. It isn't a word that I use every day. I don't see how the definition fits Evette."

"There are lots of instances, but here's an example. One day, when she was obviously upset about something, I gave her a 'Jesus loves you' sticker and smiley face. Good, right? I thought so, too. So did Evette. She waited for me outside of my trig class. Evette hugged me, and said, 'Thanks for caring.' *But*, when the same scenario repeated itself a week later, Evette threw the smiley face into the trash and stomped off."

"That's odd. Hmm, you don't know why? Well, maybe the second problem was more serious than the first one was. You know, we do have our degrees of stress."

"I don't have a clue at this point, but Evette is a tough person to figure out. Maybe I haven't tried hard enough to get to know her. I'm working on it, and I'm glad you all are here." Karen studied them with turned-down lips. "I was so sad earlier. But," she said, smiling, "even though we just escaped a rough patch, I still expect a special outcome by morning."

Sandy pointed her finger beneath Karen's nose. "Keep that mindset, cuz. I mean it. Don't let anyone or anything change your mind. When I talked to Linda Tuesday, she said Evette was unsure if she would come. Then yesterday, Linda said the problem had been resolved, but she didn't say how. Angie, the Holy Spirit led Karen to have this pajama party."

Uneasiness filled Angela's eyes. "Hmm. This is my first time hearing about it. Why didn't you tell me, Karen?"

"I forgot, and then, I forgot that I forgot. But yeah, I believe God led me to ask the people that I invited. Believe me, I've tackled easier tasks than keeping four angry friends off my back."

Sandy stepped into the kitchen. "It's a God thing. Forget about peace with the girls not invited. I believe you made excellent choices. Of the gang, I've always liked Kathy, Lisa, and Joann the best."

Karen closed the door behind her. "Me too, although I probably shouldn't admit it."

Once inside the kitchen, Sandy placed her things on the table and headed straight to the stove. She lifted the food-warmer top. "Hot link sausages. Do you have barbecue sauce? I'm starved. I skipped dinner so I could pig out over here." Then she spied the dessert container on the counter. "Ooh, pink cupcakes. Somebody got fancy with the frosting." She grinned at Karen. "Diane?"

"I'm offended." Karen placed a hand on each hip. "What if I said that I did them?"

"Then I would know that you supplied the ingredients and Diane did the baking and icing."

Angela peeped over Sandy's shoulder. "I didn't eat dinner either. Hamburgers. I love to eat grilled meat. Especially when it's cold outside. I knew Karen would drown us in food. Let's say hi to everyone then hideout in here overeating."

"Good idea." Sandy bit into a cupcake. "Um, someone baked a delicious cupcake, and it wasn't Karen."

Karen slipped one off the tray. "Smarty. This is my fourth

cupcake, and I was trying to pace myself throughout the night. Oh well, maybe tomorrow."

"Try next week," said Angela. "You have a ton of food here, girl."

Sandy swiped another cupcake from the container. "I'll take half of everything home with me in the morning. Especially these scrumptious cupcakes. I need a plate."

"First say hi to the others, then eat," said Karen. She moved to the door. "Everyone stashed their stuff by the front hall closet. Bring your things into the family room if you want to. I'm going to check on everybody."

* * *

"See you in a few," Sandy told her cousin's back. She removed a bottle of barbeque sauce from the refrigerator, then set it down on the counter. Next she picked up a foam plate from the stack and went straight to the stove, and lifted the top to the food warmer. "Mmm ... my sandwich is going to taste delicious. I can't wait to eat. Oh ..." She spun around with the top in her hand. "Did I promise not to eat now or did Karen suggest that I shouldn't?"

"Nice try. Karen said to wait, and you technically agreed. Before she left, you didn't say you were going to eat anyway." She took the lid out of Sandy's hand and replaced it back on the food warmer. "It'll be easier for you to resist eating if you stop staring at the food." Although she looked at her friend, her thoughts appeared to be far away.

Sandy watched her back and started to speak, but then she decided to wait.

Why anticipate what she's going to say when I can just let her say it?

"I don't think I'll say anything to the others about my breakup with Jeff. They'll all find out soon enough." She hitched her thumbs into the belt loops on her jeans. "Do you think they already know?"

Sandy searched for the right response. She wanted Angela to relax and enjoy herself at the party. It was past time for her friend to stop thinking about Jeff. They broke up three days ago. He'd been a part of her life way too long.

How can I help her to forget Jeff and get on with her life? She'll be happier without him. But should I say that?

She put down the cupcake she held. "It doesn't matter whether they know or not. Anyway, like you said, everyone will find out soon enough. Jeff messed up. You didn't. Remember that." She squeezed her friend's arm and smiled. "Angie, you did the right thing by breaking it off."

"I know, but it still hurts. News does travel fast in some circles, though. Three guys asked me for a date today."

"You said ..."

"No. On Wednesday my mother told me to spend time with my friends for a while. That life will look different without Jeff hanging around. I hope she's right."

Sandy picked up her cupcake. "That sounds like wise advice to me. Wish I'd said it."

"I wish I'd thought it. Instead, I felt sorry for myself." She took her cell phone from her pocket and followed Sandy out of the room. "Better call my mom and let her know we're here. Why does Karen want us to turn off our cell phones?"

Sandy set her gear on the floor and fished through her purse for her cell phone.

That's a good question I forgot to ask her. I'll try to figure it out for myself tonight without bringing it up.

"Thanks for the reminder. I think she doesn't want us to have any outside distractions while we're here."

"Hmm, that could be good or bad. Which one is it? Stop the

pretense. You know that you know what your cousin is up to. So spill it."

"I'm clueless this time. Really," she said when Angela squinted at her. "Go ahead, call your mom before Karen accuses us of eating since we haven't joined them in the family room."

Chapter Nine

The makeovers were done when Karen rejoined the party. Joann polished Kathy's fingernails. Diane practiced dance steps with Linda. Evette thumbed through a fashion magazine, while she munched on watermelon wedges. Lisa sat off by herself and worked a logic problem.

Maybe her friend would solve the teaser that had stumped Karen for days. She hoped so, because she never worked on another problem unless she solved the previous puzzle.

She moved farther into the room. This ambiance was just what she had waited for. Peace filled the atmosphere. All was well.

Yes!

Karen eyed Joann and swiftly walked across the room. "Stop polishing Kathy's fingernails. I ... demand ... my ... facial. Forget the manicure. Brenda gave me one yesterday." She shuddered at the fingernail she'd bitten off earlier, picked up the two-tier makeup case, and sat down with it on her lap.

Joann took the makeup kit from Karen's hand. "I didn't pack up my supplies. You're next, after I finish with Kathy's nails. I'm almost done." She studied Karen's mouth through narrowed eyes. "Pick out a lip gloss that isn't a neutral shade. I'm tired of looking at your colorless lips."

Karen puckered her lips, kissing the air. "My mouth is kissable without wearing a tinted shade. Too bad I don't have a boy to kiss."

Joann laughed. "Wearing a tinted shade might lure in the perfect guy. Boys ask you out despite those bare lips."

"Tinted lips? Nix that idea for a fix," said Kathy. "The perfect guy is already standing in the wings. He wants to be noticed."

Karen inched close to her. "Who is he? Don't drop a bombshell and then go silent."

Kathy inspected her fingernails once Joann said she was done. "Thanks. My hands look great."

"Hurry up. Stop stalling. Spit it out," said Karen.

"Um, maybe this is the right time to tell you. I was looking for the perfect moment to spring him on you." Kathy looked excited. Her caramel-colored skin glowed. She peeked at Karen from underneath her bangs. "Joey's best buddy is the real deal, the boy you've been waiting to date. You two will be great together. Catch her, Jo. She seems woozy."

Karen scooted in front of Joann to get her makeover started before she spoke. It was hard to form her words. "Butch Hayes and me? No way. We're too much alike. Besides, I've known him forever. We used to crawl around in diapers whenever our mothers got together."

"Rethink that thought. Butch is the boy for you. Stop thinking of him as just another friend." Kathy lowered her voice to set the mood. "He's rugged, intelligent, *and* a nice guy. That's the type of guy you're attracted to. Plus, he likes you. A lot."

Kathy studied Karen's shocked expression before she continued. "Why do you think he hangs around you all the time? Butch always rides me about setting up you two on a double date with Joey and me. You didn't have a clue, did you?"

"No, I didn't. Butch never gave away how he felt."

"He hides his feelings *way* too much. That's why I tease him whenever a guy asks you for a date. I told him each time a boy asked you out. Butch keeps on me to set something up, and I always put him off, but I'll stop if you're interested."

"You expect an answer, now? You just sprang this on me."

Kathy placed her fingers on Karen's knee. "He's a good guy. I don't want to see him get hurt."

"Me neither. Butch and I are friends. That's why we hang out together."

"Evidently he wants to be more than a friend," Joann said. "Do you like him? Don't say you like all your friends."

"That's a crazy question. Of course I like Butch. He knows that. We share similar interests. We like the same games, movies, and book types. Except for music. He has horrible taste in music." She grimaced, and then she looked happy as she grinned. "Besides that one fault we always have loads of stuff to talk about. We're tight with each other's families, too. His mother ropes me into taking his sisters clothes shopping. Butch takes Jason to the barber shop whenever my father is out of town."

"Clothes shopping. No wonder those girls are dressing better. Ouch," Joann said. She rubbed her arm where Karen pinched her. "Okay, I'll say nice things about the Hayes family."

"You'd better. They're some of my favorite people. Hmm, I never considered Butch as a potential date." She squinted at Kathy. "I'm confused ... why didn't he just ask me out?"

"You treat him like a buddy instead of a possible boyfriend." Kathy sighed at Karen's blank expression. "You two talk about your families and church events. Neither of you brings up personal topics other than family."

"And—"

"Be reasonable," said Joann. "Think about the situation from his side. If he'd asked you for a date and you'd said no, a good friendship might've been ruined."

"I am not a heartless person. He knows that."

"But you are very self-contained," said Linda. "I bet that half of the people who think they know you, don't. At least not as well as they imagine they do."

"Wait, I'm trying to find the holes in that statement, but you might be right. Okay, what Joann said does make sense. It would've been awkward for both of us if I'd rejected him."

"Also for your families," said Kathy. "I understand why he sent out feelers first."

The silent girls mulled over the new development. Joann remembered the makeover, and selected a cherry shade of lipstick and gold lip gloss.

Diane threw a potato chip at Karen to get her attention. "Do you remember when I told you Butch watches you wherever you go? You two will look great together. Look at the bonuses. No 'getting to know one another' hassles, nor awkward family moments with each other's parents. Sounds good to me. Who else do he and Joey pal around with besides Sandy's boyfriend?"

"Trey Morgan and Skip Hunter," said Evette. She blushed then turned away.

Diane started to reply but hesitated. She glanced at Karen before she looked inquisitively at Evette.

"Which boy do you like, Evette? Trey or Skip?" Karen asked.

No answer. The only boy I've seen Evette talking to is Sandy's boyfriend, Chris. Which boy did Evette like?

"Don't forget Cody Kennedy and Danny Riley. Cody has his eye on you-know-who, but Danny is fun. He broke up with his girl. They're closer friends to Joey and Butch than Chris is. Trey and Skip are Chris's friends."

Karen observed Evette's reaction. Then she noticed Kathy studied Evette, too.

Yeah, something's up. Kathy and I can compare notes later.

Karen tore her gaze away from Evette to focus on Kathy. "Yes, I'd like to date Butch if the offer is still open. Our folks will be surprised, but, then again, maybe not. What do you think, Lisa?"

"You say the guys who ask you out can't compete with Butch. That he does everything better than any boy you know."

"But I meant as a friend. Hmm ... Yeah, I guess I do compare every guy to him. Butch Hayes and Karen Duncan. You're right. I think our names go well together."

Lisa fanned herself. "Aw—Isn't he related to your pastor?"

"Yep, they're cousins. I'll fall in love if he's anything like Pastor Scott. The man is awesome."

"We're here," said Angela. She stepped into the room with Sandy, set her purse on a shelf and stored her gear in a corner. "I agree." She grabbed a handful of potato chips from the bowl she passed. "Pastor Scott's the best. He'll marry his childhood sweetheart before Christmas. He and Beth make a great team."

Joann slid the makeup kit in front of Karen. "It's about time you all got here," she said without looking up.

Angela ambled up beside her. "Are we late for something special?"

"No, you're not." Diane scooted over. "Sit next to me." She waved over the girl who popped a last bite of cupcake into her mouth. "Sandy, sit here. Where's your sleeping bag? Did you leave it the hallway?"

Sandy moved closer to the group as she licked frosting from her fingers. "Who knows where it is. I lent it to Jason last summer." Her eyes widened. "Karen, did he take my sleeping bag to his friend's house? Does Brenda still have her pink one?"

"I bet he did. I didn't think about him taking yours with him when he left for school. The pink sleeping bag should be in the attic somewhere. We'll grab it later."

Angela sat beside Diane then made room for Sandy to sit

between them. "We heard the conversation from the hallway. My mother was slow coming to the phone, and I couldn't bring the cell phone in here. I agree with you. 'Karen and Butch' sounds good together. What is his real name? I've always called him Butch."

Dimples highlighted Karen's face. She couldn't stop grinning. "Andrew Michael Hayes the Second. Butch is named after his grandfather." She picked up the toner bottle Joann had set down to read the ingredients. "Oh, Sandy, before I forget, did you take the swim team pictures before you left school?"

Her cousin plopped on the floor between Angela and Diane. "I barely made it to the gym before they left. I'll snap more pictures at the meet tomorrow. I'm out of there by three regardless of how many shots I've taken. It'll be too crowded to move around after that. Imagine five counties descending on Shiatown in one day."

"Don't remind me about tomorrow," said Lisa. "I had planned to watch Kevin compete before the game started, but relatives from out of town dropped in on my grandmother this afternoon. It was a surprise visit, so we're having a family reunion tomorrow. My mother won't let me skip time with relatives to attend the swim meet and perform at the game."

Joann wiped a wet cotton ball over Karen's cheeks. "Stop frowning. Keep still." She tossed the cotton ball into the wastebasket and picked up a makeup sponge. "Parents need to give their teens more freedom. My folks are never in sync with me. Of course, I'm always right."

"Unless you're wrong," said Kathy. "My parents understand me perfectly, so they limit my activities. My mom said, 'We're saving you from yourself.' I like that."

"It sounds like a conspiracy to me," said Linda. "My dad said the same thing last weekend. He keeps trying to ruin my social life. Three of my friends wanted me to spend the night with them in Tulsa after the game Saturday."

"Your parents are different from my folks. They would laugh if I asked to spend a night out of town with friends without a chaperone. I'm not allowed to ask them pointless questions," said Diane. "Did you expect them to say yes? Did the other girls stay overnight?"

"Two of them did, and they convinced three other girls to join them."

"Unbelievable. They're underage to get a hotel room. Someone had to get the room for them. Five parents allowed their teenage daughters to spend the night unsupervised in Tulsa. Doing what?" asked Angela.

"Mainly shopping. They had a great time from all accounts. I'm still jealous." She addressed Lisa. "Maybe you can watch Kevin compete, do your color guard thing at the game, then attend the reunion afterwards. Won't that make everyone happy?"

"Not my folks. They said no, and they mean what they say. Anyway, Kevin won't tell me our school's start time. He's angry that I can't come, as if I decide where and when I can go. Who cares. I'm getting tired of Kevin. It'll be okay."

"You hope," said Joann. "Logic hasn't caught up with Nick. It's countdown time. I gave him the official five-day warning Wednesday."

"Every boy gets a five-day warning after the first date with you. You're going to run out of guys to date at that rate," said Kathy.

Joann set the sponge on the towel. "Look, I have this process down pat. The first date lets me know if I want a second one. Sometimes I can't decide until I reach my house. Mainly it depends on whether they respect my space. I don't like touchy-feely stuff at all. If they pass that hurdle, I expect to be wooed into the second date."

Linda winced. "Ouch, that hurt. I bit my tongue." She sipped her drink then focused on Joann. "Wooed, huh? Isn't that word a little antiquated?"

"Not to me. I expect old-fashioned respect and won't accept anything less—from anybody."

Chapter Ten

"Not even a kiss?" asked Linda.

"No. I don't let a guy hold my hand on the first date. My mother was right about this one, and I respect her advice. Man-handle me, and it's over for good. Those limits are non-negotiable, and I won't defend my position. I'm not sleeping with any man except for my husband, and I won't kiss every boy I date. That rule is written in the stone of my mind. I don't want multiple men *knowing* me."

Linda seemed disappointed with the explanation. "That's cool. But you do realize you're in the minority with that opinion. Not everyone thinks that way."

"I do," said Kathy, "that's why I hang out with Joey. Kind of, sort of dating a friend is great. We protect each other from anyone we don't like asking us out. I hate to explain myself."

"Hold up," said Linda. "Are you saying that you and Joey aren't a genuine item? He just protects you from boys who want to date you?"

"It works both ways. Most girls think Joey is hot and won't leave him alone. He's safe with me."

Linda immediately pointed out what she called lies. "Being deceptive is wrong, even if you have good intentions."

Karen thought the couple liked each other more than they let on. Her heart swelled with pride. She enjoyed hearing the group debate the pros and cons of sexual purity. To know that Joann still practiced the "no sex before marriage" promise pleased her. The gang had adopted the stance in eighth grade after a girl at school got pregnant. Some of their crowd had repeatedly reneged and had loads of regrets. Not that any of them had set out to break the vow. Only, after it happened the first time, the boys who asked them out expected to have sex with them. It was sad to hear that the girls had mostly given in. That was why Joanne's announcement mattered. To hear the promise declared to others encouraged Karen.

Lots of us are out in the open and unafraid of being teased for our beliefs.

Angela went to the table and grabbed a handful of potato chips. "Your skin is glowing. Show me the new CDs before Joann does your makeup. I'll get them myself if they're in the cabinet."

Diane mashed her lips together. "Oh no. Not music again."

"Did Sandy and I miss something?" Angela asked. "We probably missed a lot by coming late."

"Just a brief discussion on my music preferences," Karen said. "I think my choices surprised a few people."

Angela removed the CD case from the cabinet and settled next to Evette. A smile played on her lips while she rifled through the collection. "For the record, I like your selections. I have most of these same CDs at home."

"Well, I don't, and I'll tell you why," Joann said.

Karen ignored Joann's latest rant. She sifted through Linda's views about premarital sex. Her belief that her position held the majority baffled Karen. Loads of folks abstained from having sex until they married. Many were followers of Christ, but some had other reasons.

Linda had defended her position and never said she was a participant. But the eager defense of birth control for teens and safe sex slotted her. Karen hated Linda's resistance to another viewpoint besides her own. It seemed Christians weren't the only people that opposed alternative lifestyles.

In eighth grade, Karen took the "no sex pledge" to fit in with her friends. Today, she cherished her ability to do the right thing instead of following the crowd. Privately, she thanked her parents that she couldn't date until her sixteenth birthday. Now she stood firm in her own belief that premarital sex was wrong.

Her pastor was young and cool and kept up with the times. Reading scripture convinced Karen that Pastor Scott had spoken the truth. All of God's decrees were correct, whether she believed them or not. No one had the right to pick and choose which rules to obey. Disobedience to God's word meant having eternal complications. Karen didn't want that outcome for herself or for anyone.

Someone saying, "Pay attention, Karen," brought her back to the party. How much of the conversation had she missed?

"Let's change the subject. I want to know what Sandy is writing," said Diane. She peered over Sandy's shoulder, to watch her scribble on a notepad.

"It's a poem I began writing at lunch. I jotted down a few keywords. Only now, I can't remember what I had in mind."

Diane leaned in for a better look. "I didn't know you wrote poetry. How many poems have you written so far?"

"Six. It's my little secret. Well, it was until now." Sandy looked at the other girls, then she closed the tablet and laid it beside her. "I started this hobby last week. They're not good enough for anyone else to read, but I'll keep trying."

"I bet your poems are better than you think they are. It's impossible to judge your own work. Let us critique each one for you."

Sandy took a long minute to make up her mind. She seemed

about to give in, but then she shook her head. She peeked at Karen's bland face, and once Karen smiled, she relented. "All right, but remember I'm a novice at writing poetry. No laughing, agreed?" She paused for a moment. "I don't see any heads nodding." She looked at each face until every girl nodded her head in agreement. "I always get nervous when I expose myself to criticism." She cleared her throat as she picked up the poems. "Okay, ooh ... here we go."

> *What will it take to turn you on*
> *to the truth that Jesus Christ is Lord?*
> *This is what I've decided to do.*
> *Rejoice and share His good news with you.*
> *I'll turn down sounds of worldly noise.*
> *I'll proclaim praises to my Lord.*
> *I'll do away with token strokes.*
> *I'll shout aloud, He's the Lord of Hosts.*

Sandy passed the tablet to the eager Diane. "Here, you read the next one."

Diane rose to her knees as she scanned the page. "Good. I get to go first. Some of these are Christian poems ... I'm ready."

> *Okay, keep having everything your way.*
> *You're refusing to listen to whatever I say.*
> *But no person can chart their own course.*
> *Living in sin without showing remorse.*
> *Who knows how many people the Lord has sent.*
> *To show you the areas in which you must repent.*

"I think the poem is good. There are four poems left. Angela, I want you to take a turn. Karen is next."

Karen winked at her cousin before she accepted the book from Diane. "*Whispers* is the title."

> *As I walked into the room, all eyes turned my way.*
> *The hooded glances and knowing looks were enough*
> *   to ruin my day.*
> *What could be the cause?*
> *Oh! Have I offended them all?*
> *Of course, this could never be.*
> *None of these people are known to me.*

Lisa smiled. "That poem sounds like Sandy wrote it."

"I get the meaning. There's no improvement needed," Karen said. She passed the tablet to Evette. "Your turn."

The startled girl's eyes widened as she took the notepad. Evette read the poem to herself before she read it out loud. "This one is titled *Thanksgiving*."

> *Believe God for everything. Praise Him indeed.*
> *But don't allow your dreams to turn into greed.*
> *For the scope of His blessings are both great and small.*
> *Father God it is You we must thank for them all.*

Evette reflected on the words then handed off to Joann.

Karen gritted her teeth when Joann accepted the notepad. She wanted her to concentrate on the makeover. She tried to view her face in a hand-held mirror. "You've been working on me for twenty minutes. Finish up after you read this poem."

"Hush, I'm excited to be asked to read out loud. Thank you, Evette. *Was It Something I Said?* Not me," Joann said with a laugh, "that's the title."

How can her troubles be my fault?
I only said, "Her dress is too short."
I never revealed she stays out all night.
At home she entertains every man in sight.
In walks one guy, out walks another.
There was Leon, James, and even James's brother.
I never told that her children play outside until dawn.
Or how she openly wishes that they were never born.
So out of all the things I could've relayed,
the remark I made was both harmless and staid.
Okay, so my comment caused people to look
at her life as though it was an open book.
But still I contend there's no way I'm to blame
for a bunch of nosey folks out to defame.

"That's a live one *and* it's quite true," Angela said. "Believe me, I know. I like it. Submit the poem to The Poet's Corner at the bookstore."

"Is that a Christian poem?" Diane asked while doubtfully shaking her head.

"It's a people poem," said Sandy. "To me, this poem is a lesson against hurting others. It's good to speak the truth in love to the person involved. This poem is about gossip. Rumors can destroy someone's life forever. Attention is called to a person whenever we talk about their behavior, their attitudes, who they are." She spread her hands while she explained, but struck Diane's face as Diane leaned toward her. Sandy rubbed the girl's cheek with her fingers. "Excuse me. Are you okay?"

Diane patted the side of her face. "I am, but that right hook is lethal."

Amusement entered Sandy's expression. She parted her lips to speak but hesitated. "What was I saying? Oh yeah. Sometimes we don't notice people until someone else brings up their name. If the comment is harmful, then our impression of the person can be negative. The woman was placed in a no-win situation."

Diane seemed unconvinced by the explanation. She still observed Sandy. "You're next, Angela."

Joann passed the notepad to Angela.

"I'm looking forward to reading this one," Angela said. "Let's see ..."

Listen, the Lord is speaking to you.
Let His word possess you anew.
Do you hear the gentle promptings of the Holy Spirit?
Rest in His perfect peace.
Enjoy freedom from internal riots.
Open your ears. Still your soul. Quiet. Quiet. Quiet.
Do you hear the gentle promptings of the Holy Spirit?

As soon as she finished speaking, Kathy clapped her hands to get everyone's attention.

"I like your poems. But ... I didn't expect to hear *Was It Something I Said.* Don't act surprised. You always preach about keeping your thought life pure. In order to rhyme about the woman being a slut, you had to think about it first."

"The poem speaks for *itself,*" Karen said. She emphasized the last word. That was her and Kathy's agreed-upon hint whenever either one wanted the other one to back off.

"Uh-uh. You know Sandy always says, 'I don't think trashy thoughts.' So how did she write that poem without it first coming to her mind?"

Sandy pointed a finger beneath her chin. "Me, write trash? Are you serious? The poem exposes the harmful effects of gossip.

The person added fuel to the fire. They ramped it up and didn't allow the previous rumors to die out."

"Everyone listens to rumors," said Lisa. "Besides, it isn't gossip if it's true."

Sandy laughed. "Where did you get that definition from? Not Merriam-Webster."

"No, smarty, an online dictionary. I like being well-informed."

Sandy wiped moisture from her eyes. "Well-informed? This is about gossip, not definitions. Are you … admitting that you're nosey?"

"Swap that word with newsy, and I'll confess. Seriously," said Linda, "I like to learn about current events. Most people do."

Angela's hand shook when she laughed. Lemonade dripped from the cup she lifted to her mouth. She grabbed napkins off the table and wiped the drink off her jeans. "Stop making me laugh. Current events. I like that talking point."

Linda eyed Angela. "Clue me in on what's making you laugh. I want to laugh too. What's funny about current events?"

"I guess it depends on your definition of the word. I halfway agree with you, though. Rumor mongers are great listeners and quick to spread the news. However, no one has the right to destroy another person's reputation. If it's illegal, report it. If it's immoral, you can try to talk to them about it. Don't forget, you can always pray."

Linda laid flat on her stomach. "Nothing's that simple when you deal with people, and you know that. Life doesn't work according to our wishes, Angie. Sometimes people tell me in-formation that I don't want to hear. Loose-lipped people are everywhere you go."

"No one can feed you garbage unless you decide to eat it. I was taught in elementary school to walk away if you don't want to listen."

Linda beckoned the other girls. "Feel free to jump in at any time." She peered at Angela before she sat up. "We both know life isn't that easy. I don't blow off people if I can avoid it."

"It's important for me to be me and not to act like I'm you," said Sandy. "I stay away from people who won't accept the real me. The price is much too high to pay to someone that isn't my friend."

"That's very unrealistic with the teenagers I know. If the person has other good qualities, shouldn't we overlook one character flaw? No one is perfect," said Evette.

"That's true, but we identify with the people we hang around with the most," Karen said. "We have lots of things in common with our friends."

Evette's alert gaze pinpointed Karen, and Karen's heart sank.

Oops, why did I say that? I left myself wide open for an attack, and here it comes.

Chapter Eleven

"You do?" asked Evette. "I mean … you believe that we think like our friends. If so, I'm shocked that you admit it so freely. Your friends gossip all the time. They're backbiting experts."

Lisa leaned back on her elbows. "Gossipers? Who are you talking about?"

Evette eyed Lisa. "If the bed is yours, then lie in it. If not, don't be defensive."

That attack came out of nowhere. I thought all had been forgiven after Lisa apologized. Let it go, Lisa. Here, I'll help you.

"I can only speak for myself," said Karen. "Not too long ago, I couldn't keep anything secret. I guess that made me a gossiper. Now, I leave if the conversation goes south."

Joann noisily snapped the cap on the cotton ball container. "Do-gooder Karen. The crazy talk takes away my concentration from your makeover."

The remark cut into Karen's heart as was probably intended. She squeezed her finger to keep quiet. *How can Joann apply makeup to my face and mock me at the same time? I'm finally tempted to send her home for real.*

Diane left her spot to kneel beside Karen. "Classy as usual. A little do-gooding never hurt anyone." She stared at Joann as if daring her to speak. "Anything would be a great improvement. Your attitude sucks. You talk more trash than any person I know."

"This is the second time you've spoken up for Karen tonight. Her tongue is sharp. She can defend herself." Joanne picked up a lipstick tube, and pointed it at Diane. "Stay out of my business."

Sandy abandoned her notepad and leaned forward. "The old Karen took shots at everyone, but not anymore." She smiled at Joann. "She's working on it because she's tired of acting childish."

Linda flopped onto her back. "We're way off track. Back to the original conversation. Angela, some friends require more help than others. You don't run away from your friends when they need you the most."

"None of us are equipped to handle each other's problems," Angela said, "even if we want to help. It's hard enough to make the right choices for me. I don't help my friends if I dish out the wrong advice."

A saddened Evette lifted her hand into the air as if she were in a classroom. "So we're supposed to ignore their need, just walk away from the relationship. Believe me, that's the outcome if you blow off a friend when they need your support."

"No. That's not what I'm saying. Why would I dish out bad advice to people I like? Jesus is the problem-solver few people want to know. We all need His help to make it."

Linda shook her head so hard it should've hurt. "Uh-uh. I'm not buying your empty comments tonight. Forget eternity. Everyone needs real solutions to their problems. Answers that work in the here and now."

"I don't know about you," said Sandy, "but God has always been there for me and my family. Life is hard. To live without godly principles makes it even harder."

Suddenly, Linda appeared to be angry. Even her breathing seemed to increase. "Don't feed me those lies. Christians do whatever they please, and then they blame the fallout on a being no one can hold accountable. You call it living a godly life. My dad calls it smoke and mirrors."

"On that note, it's time for a break." Joann stood up, checked her watch, and looked at Karen. "All done."

Karen studied her face in a mirror. She set it aside and stuck her hand in the popcorn bowl.

"Admit that you look beautiful," Joann said. She checked her watch again. "*Parallel Worlds* starts in ten minutes. Your bedroom?"

Now how do I say no politely? I don't watch paranormal stuff, especially in my bedroom. But Joann has blown hot and cold all evening. Accepting no isn't likely to happen with her tonight.

"Sure, Joann, but this is an important discussion. Why leave now? If you didn't record it at home, watch it online tomorrow. It's on their website."

"Jesus talk is why I'm out of here. I can tell the topic won't change soon enough for me to stay." She glanced at the other girls watching her and Karen. "Does anyone else want to see the show?"

"Not me. I never watch supernatural stuff," said Lisa.

Karen nodded at her. "Good for you. No one should open up the door to the spirit world."

"I'm sick of how you think you know what everyone else should do," Joann said. She stalked across the room, but stopped at the door.

"Go on, suit yourself," said Karen. "But those programs are a trick from the devil."

Joann tapped her toe on the floor. "Okay, how is that?"

Karen noticed Kathy's finger wriggling at her. Once the girl mouthed the words, "Stand your ground," Karen balanced on her knees. "I'll set the scenario for you. Imagine if you watch something unworldly, then find yourself in a similar situation. It can produce anxiety that might develop into fear." She smiled and plonked onto the floor. "We studied phobias in health class last year."

"The book said phobias are a trick from the devil? I don't think so," said Linda.

Karen glanced at her. "He wasn't mentioned. But I know two plus two equals four and not eight. I learned that in kindergarten. So did you."

"Me too," said Lisa. "I've experienced strange situations before. I hated that I was frightened by any of them."

"Many people don't realize the truth," said Sandy. "There is a spiritual world that's active, alive, and very interested in us."

Lisa shivered. "You mean *Parallel World* is real? I don't even want to think about that."

Sandy nodded. "Most people ignore, mock, or treat it as a fantasy. Some folks even die before they ever lived. My mom says that fear of anything is an entrance into the spirit world no one needs to take. That we should avoid opening doors for our enemy to harass us later."

"I like your mother, Sandy, but, enemy? Are you talking about the devil?" Joann checked her watch for the third time. "It's nine-thirty. Tell me about this enemy later. I might listen for a change." She left the room before Sandy replied. Diane, Evette, and Linda trooped out the door behind her.

Inside the family room, the girls listened to Joann as she headed down the hallway.

"Can you believe Karen and Sandy used fear as a weapon to get their way?"

Karen waited for the response but didn't hear their reply. The group had moved beyond earshot of the door. She should've anticipated Joann's typical reaction whenever God was mentioned. But, Diane and Evette opting to watch the series surprised Karen.

Diane hated those types of shows. Evette's expression revealed she disliked them as well. Yet both girls chose to join Joann. Their willingness to leave when they appeared to want to stay defied logic. Particularly with Diane. She'd fought with Joann all evening, yet she chose to follow behind her.

Kathy sighed loudly. "So discussing Jesus is the way to a clear room. Not for me. I like having talks that improve my life."

Lisa chewed popcorn as she lounged on the floor. "Jesus is the problem-solver. I heard someone else say that before tonight." She dusted crumbs off her fingers. "Angie, did Jesus solve your problems with Jeff? I heard a rumor before I left school today. They *say* you're no longer a couple. Did the gossipers get it right this time?"

Angela flinched and hung her head. Her hand pushed forward like someone who held off an attack.

A light bulb went off for Karen. Now she understood the girl's strange behavior when they talked inside the garage. Her attitude changed once Sandy mentioned the Holy Spirit. Did she think the Holy Spirit would uncover what had happened between her and Jeff? It seemed that Angela wanted to lay low tonight. She didn't want to talk about Jeff. Based on Sandy's comment, she'd thought his name might crop up.

"I think Lisa hit a sore spot," said Kathy. "If so, don't answer the question. It's none of our business. We can keep our conversation general. Specifics aren't a requirement."

"That's okay. It hurts, and the pain is real. My mom believes time will heal the ache if I let God heal me. I'm glad the other girls left the room. I can speak more freely without them. Sandy already knows everything that happened with Jeff."

She took a deep breath. "Whew, what can I say? I knew Jeff and I were destined for failure, but I dismissed those thoughts at the same time. I liked the fact that the boy every girl wanted preferred me."

"Join the club. Most people like having their ego stroked," said Karen.

"My father calls it self-indulgence. He said to expect a bad outcome each time I ignore the warning signs. Believe me, the alarm always rang."

Lisa shifted position. "So what happened to break you up?"

Angela swept a blond lock behind her ear. She focused her gaze on Sandy. "I won't hide the truth from you. Anyway, the entire story will leak out soon enough. Jeff got a girl at another school pregnant."

"What?" asked Kathy, wide-eyed. "You're kidding."

"Wish I was. I can't fake surprise that it happened. Sometimes I wondered if he slept around. But I think it was a case of 'better some other girl than me'."

Lisa and Kathy traded glances. "In what way?" Lisa asked before she peeked at Karen.

"Jeff never hassled me to have sex with him. That made it easy to pretend we had the perfect relationship."

"Ah," said Lisa, "you let him date other girls so he wouldn't hound you?"

Lisa, look at Angela blush. You could have phrased your comment better than that.

Lisa slid away from Karen after Karen elbowed her in the side. "Well? Was that why you did it?"

Angela twiddled her thumbs on her lap. "Sort of, but not really. Ignoring the signs seemed an excellent solution for us. As far as I know, Jeff only dated me. No one has told me that they've seen him out with another girl."

She drank her lemonade and placed the empty cup beside her.

"Jeff and I went everywhere together for four years. He

seemed satisfied with a goodnight kiss. Yeah, sometimes I wondered if he fooled around. I still can't believe he might've had unprotected sex and didn't use birth control."

Kathy sat up. "Something's wrong with that picture. Jeff could take care of having unprotected sex himself. But did he always use that method when he did? If so, did he use it correctly every time? Yet that's not the real issue here. Would protection against STDs and pregnancy make everything okay? You and Jeff were exclusive. He disrespected the relationship."

"I won't offer excuses for him or myself. I know my attitude was wrong. Doing the right thing matters, even if you never get caught. I repeatedly ignored the truth. Maybe I didn't want to know. If I did, I would have had to reach a decision. It hurt too much to examine my own beliefs. Although, lying to myself didn't work. I'm forced to deal with the consequences either way."

"Isn't he a Christian?" asked Lisa. "He hangs out with the God crowd at school."

"Thank you," Karen said. "That's the question I wanted to ask."

If Jeff led a double life, then my vote is no, he doesn't know God. But everyone makes mistakes, even people who know God. The key is to stop making those mistakes.

Angela shrugged her shoulders. "Who knows? Jeff goes to church on Sundays. He even goes to youth meeting every Wednesday. But he hangs outside and skateboard with his friends all evening. I messed up big time. I dismissed his actions and refused to confront him."

"That's over," said Sandy. "You repented. God forgave you. It's time to move on."

Angela rolled onto her stomach then buried her face on her arm.

Karen felt like doing the same thing. This was serious stuff.

Had she treated the night too lightly? *I don't know what I expected to happen, but it wasn't this. Nothing's working out as I'd planned. Half of the girls are watching a series that I hate in my bedroom. Ugh!*

Angela spoke without raising her head. "I had a big talk with my parents. They were clueless about how rebellious Jeff can be. Some of his escapades truly surprised them. I let my parents down."

Sandy reached her hand into the popcorn bowl Lisa had discarded. "Thank God, He hears our prayers, answers them, and He forgives us when we repent. The hard part is to forgive ourselves for the mess up. That's difficult to do if we repeat those same mistakes."

"What about the girl?" asked Karen. "As usual, she'll pay a higher price than Jeff."

Chapter Twelve

"I only know her name. Jeff was candid with me about the conversation with his parents. His father's reaction was a big surprise. He said he was glad that Jeff didn't want a permanent relationship with the girl. 'Never marry your mistakes,' he said. I guess she'll be pretty much on her own."

"Of course she's on her own. Jeff doesn't work," said Kathy, visibly disgusted.

Angela turned onto her back and crossed a leg over her knee. "Jeff is a good guy in most ways. Too bad he takes his alter ego wherever he goes. We had little in common, but I hung on anyway—even putting up with his arrogant friends. They were a package deal." She sat up again and combed fingers through her hair. "We broke up Wednesday. I'm sad *and* happier without him. Why did I waste four years not dating other guys?"

She reached out her hand to Lisa. "I know Kevin is different from Jeff, but don't get stuck with someone out of habit. Be careful."

Karen's gaze swept over her friend. Many people had given Lisa the same advice about her boyfriend. Maybe what happened to Angela would help her reach the decision to let him go.

They've been together for a long time, so it won't be easy. Habits are hard to break—even bad ones.

"I will." Lisa massaged her thumb and forefinger across her

chin. She picked up a jack with her other hand. When she looked up, her expressionless face shouted out the struggle within her. "He's too possessive. Joann mentioned it the other day, as did several other friends."

Sandy jumped up so quickly she almost lost her balance. "Living each day is a challenge. Boyfriend troubles makes it worse. Everything about Chris confuses me most of the time. My stomach just growled. I'm starved. Let's leave our problems here and hit the kitchen. We have tons of food."

* * *

Linda sat with her legs crossed at the ankle, oblivious to the television screen. Hunkered on the floor against the wall, she had forgotten which show was on. The picture loomed before her, but instead of paying attention, she rehashed the discussion in the family room. She squashed her anger and studied the girl whose comments still bothered her. How could someone as popular as Joann not be sexually active?

Boys flocked around her wherever she went, drooling, no less. With guys, her beauty eclipsed her objectionable behavior. Linda had supposed they received compensation in other ways. She'd been wrong about that, and it shook her up. The Ice Princess had refused to sleep with any boy she dated. She didn't even kiss some of them. Somehow her old friend's virginity status bothered her. She felt used.

Also, Kathy's confession that she and Joey were only pals had floored Linda. The two friends had joined forces so no one else would pester them for dates. What sane person did that? The girl was the co-captain of the varsity cheerleaders. The first sophomore to ever attain that position at their school. Kathy had status none of Linda's friends had achieved. She wasn't having sex? Joey had been Kathy's boyfriend for four years. How could they not be sleeping together? Maybe they were just buddies.

It was obvious that her friends knew about the deception. Had Sandy, Diane, and Angela known about the con? Evette was the only person that Linda knew was innocent. The fake couple had fooled everyone else with their lies.

So Kathy and Joann were virgins. What about the other girls? Linda couldn't tell based on their previous conversation. The pros and cons had gone back and forth without anyone else declaring their stance.

No doubt Sandy practiced abstinence. Lisa had nodded in agreement while Joann talked. Neither Karen nor Diane had ever dated. Evette claimed she'd never had a boyfriend on the drive to Karen's house. The discussion downstairs indicated she had her eyes on either Trey or Skip. Chris was already taken, so it couldn't be him. Both boys were okay, but probably not for Evette. Somehow, they seemed sneaky. So did Chris, even though he appeared to dote on Sandy.

Everyone knew Angela and Jeff's relationship was solid. Pure gold. The pair became *the couple* their freshman year in high school. Jeff lived in the real world. Did Angela Prentis ever join him there?

Linda chuckled when Diane almost fell off the bed onto the floor. What a joke.

Stop hiding your face and jumping around on the bed. If you're afraid to watch this show, go downstairs. You're old enough to cover your eyes without harming yourself. No wonder she can't find a date. Diane is clumsy.

Stop sending out negative vibes and thinking mean thoughts because you're unhappy.

She had chosen to expose her beliefs despite not knowing the other girls' views. No one had asked for her opinion. She had freely dished it out. She kept talking until Diane tactfully switched the subject. At this point, her position was widely known. These non-friends knew more about Linda than she did about them. The realization made her angry.

The breath that blew between her lips sounded like gasps. She scowled at Joann.

Everyone had sex before marriage these days. Everyone did except for the liars who pretended they didn't. Mainly Christians. Linda's friends were no longer virgins. Few individuals waited until they said "I do." The girls here tonight were popular and up with the times in everything else. Loads of people envied their freedom to do whatever they wanted. She'd thought of Lisa, Karen, and Joann as free spirits. Especially Kathy. Everybody did. Their old-fashioned ideas caught her off guard.

Only Sandy, Karen, and Angela were Christians. Karen was a newbie at that. Linda could've easily dismissed their beliefs had they all been Jesus people. The viewpoint of the non-Christians appeared more valid to her. On what grounds could she question their judgment?

Why did their opinion upset her so much? She didn't jump into bed with every boy she dated. Nevertheless, Joann's statement haunted her thoughts.

"I don't want multiple men *knowing* me."

Neither did Linda. Where do you draw the line? The first time with a boy was in eighth grade. Way too young, she admitted to herself, embarrassed by her age. It wasn't that she was eager to have sex. Linda had reeled from being ditched by her so-called friends. While she'd searched for a place to belong, she found herself surrounded by sexually active girls. The depressed Linda had followed the path of least resistance.

Since then, one other boy had joined the ranks. That meant she'd slept with a different boy each year. Two guys she now only saw at sports events. Linda quickly averted her eyes whenever they came face-to-face. The indifference in their gazes undid her. How could they have been so close at one time, yet ignore her now?

The first guy transferred to another school and dropped Linda. She never heard from him again. When they ran into each other at a football game, he walked past her without a word. Last year, the boy she dated hung around for six months before he dumped her. He broke up with her over the telephone. She'd heard his friends talking in the background. Another girl had caught her boyfriend's attention.

Sorrow still swamped Linda each time they passed by her with another girl. Not because she wanted them back; far from it. Seeing them holding hands with someone else brought back painful memories of being discarded. Sex had been a useless act she'd repeated until each boy had walked away. Linda never backed off first. She'd expected a lifelong relationship each time.

Lately she ignored them both as if being rejected no longer mattered. Only, it did. Joann's dissention unleashed the grief Linda seldom acknowledged. What was done couldn't be undone. There was no chance of a redo. She was stuck with her choices.

She silently sighed, and admitted the truth. Sometimes she had to physically fight off some of the guys she dated. It was difficult to date boys who'd saturated themselves with porn. Many of the boys had bragged about it. That had to be the reason why they refused to accept no for an answer, until she beat them down. For that reason, she always met her dates at an event. Linda only allowed her boyfriends to pick her up at home. The ability to use separate cars worked. But all girls didn't have that option.

Suddenly, she needed to vent. Linda wanted another ear to bounce ideas off. None of her friends would suffice for this pur-pose. Each one was mired inside the same endless pit as Linda.

They played with a fire they didn't know how to extinguish. Maybe they didn't want to.

* * *

The girls downstairs traded stories around the kitchen table. Although the conversation darted all over the place, they avoided all personal talk. Angela's breakup with Jeff cast a shadow over the party.

Karen hated Jeff's double-dealing Angela. The cause of the breakup made her sad. He had lived a double life and had never been outed. No one knew the exact year he became a cheater. Seven thousand students attended the four high schools in Shiatown. Those numbers stacked the deck against his getting caught sooner. If the girl had never gotten pregnant, Angela could've ended up married to the louse. Karen didn't dislike the boy. She could take him or leave him. He hid his bad behavior well. Even Lisa had been surprised that the rumor she'd heard was true.

Was Kevin the only boy who wanted to date one girl at a time? Thoughts of Lisa's boyfriend brought Chris to her mind. Evette's name popped up, instead of Sandy's.

Chris and Evette? Ooh, what am I thinking?

To clear her thoughts, Karen shifted her focus to Lisa. One good thing had come from Jeff's deception. In the hallway, on the way to the kitchen, Lisa had whispered, "Think I should drop Kevin?" She seemed relieved when Karen replied, "He should've been dumped ages ago." He was okay, but not for Lisa. At least not now. He expected to take up all of Lisa's free time and keep her to himself. This was an excellent time for Lisa to walk away.

Kevin refused to give Lisa the schedule for the competition because her parents said she couldn't go. Was he for real?

Karen played catch-up to join in the conversation around the table. She leaned back in her chair when Sandy said, "It isn't easy

96

for me to stay focused when I read the Bible. Sometimes I find it hard to meditate on scriptures. Too many other things grab my attention."

"How do you meditate on scripture?" asked Lisa. "Meditation reminds me of chanting and other stuff I don't do. It's sort of creepy."

"You meditate on scripture by reading the Bible daily. Consistency is the key for me," Angela said. "It's like eating healthy foods each day for better health."

Sandy nodded. "It's important to build good habits in anything worth doing."

"I've neglected to do a lot of good things. I don't read my Bible enough and I seldom eat healthy foods. Too many distractions, plus I like junk food. A mistake like dating Jeff happens when we stop doing what we know is right. I totally missed the mark on that one. My thoughts were off, and my beliefs guide my decisions."

"Yeah, new insight doesn't develop overnight," said Sandy. A light twinkled in her eyes as she turned to Karen. "One day fresh thoughts will flow through us if we learn from our mistakes. Sometimes, I don't."

"The pure-thought thing you harp on all the time?" asked Kathy.

"Uh-huh. You know I'm far from being perfect, and so do I. But I try to recognize when I do mess up. My family always sees the real me. I'm usually on my best behavior with friends and strangers. Ask Karen. She has a ringside seat to all my failures."

"I think most people are nicer to non-family members," Kathy said. "Our families will love us despite the mistakes we make. That's my reality. My family will always love me."

Angela slumped in the chair and stuffed a grape into her mouth.

"I've found out that I have to practice what I believe. Nothing else works."

"I like pleasing the people I love," said Sandy. "I love Jesus. But it's difficult to stay focused on Him. When my mind wanders my heart tries to follow where my thoughts leads."

While she listened to the conversation, a weight lifted from Karen's shoulders. Just like Kathy, she was loved and appreciated by every member of her family. Her dad loved her, yet she continually pushed him away. Was she wrong to distrust her father? It didn't matter that Brenda agreed with her if they were both wrong. Karen wanted her life laid out for her step-by-step so she couldn't make a mistake.

Lisa's knuckle popping caught her attention. Her thoughts felt far away from the conversation. It seemed her personal observations overrode what everyone else said. Now she focused on the agitated friend who sat beside her.

She wants to talk about the breakup, but she doesn't want to upset Angela. It won't. I'm sure Angie broke up with Jeff. No doubt he wanted to keep the relationship alive.

"I have a few questions to ask," Lisa said in a low voice. "Was Jeff open to being friends after you booted him? First, though, maybe I should ask if you want to stay friends with him."

"That's a good question," Karen said. "To part as friends is best unless the relationship is toxic. I think it was."

Then Lisa fired off one query after the other. Angela's responses amazed Karen. She downplayed her own pain to help Lisa to sidestep the same trap.

I called it. Kevin's history! Ooh, yes! Bye-bye!

Kathy munched on a celery stick while Angela and Lisa talked. For once, she appeared satisfied to listen until the discussion switched topics. Once that happened, her fingertips tapped a beat on the table. Her gaze went from Lisa to Karen.

Chapter Thirteen

"It isn't just Kevin. My life has changed too much. Look at my friendship with Karen. Each day my best friend acts like a stranger. I don't understand why she pulls away from me."

Karen scooted back her chair. "How can you say that? We hang out all the time. I just spent the night with you last weekend. I even went to the movies with you and Kevin."

Sandy hugged Karen when her shoulders sagged. "This is the new and improved Karen Duncan. The old version had issues." She laughed when Karen punched her on the arm.

"Does being a Christian mean we can't be friends? I want my best friend back."

Karen felt the tears well up. "Lisa—"

"That's a stupid question," Kathy said. "Where did she go? She's still here. Karen prefers to be with you more than she does with anyone else. The evidence speaks for itself. I'm surprised you're still friends with her. Your attitude proves you don't like it when she talks about God. She does that a lot. You blow her off whenever she mentions Jesus."

Angela stared at Kathy. "Like the rest of us Lisa wants to be happy. Who doesn't? The key is to search in the correct place. The Bible is right. Love, peace, and joy are only found in Jesus. I think Lisa gets the picture."

"Then why hasn't my life changed? I get the picture, too."

"Because first you have to know Jesus as your Savior," Sandy said. "Lisa's questions will help her to understand salvation."

"I don't attend church because my granny doesn't drive anymore. I need to get my driver's license so I can take her. *But,* I've always believed Jesus died on the cross and rose again. My Granny taught me when I was younger."

She hesitated then plunged into speech. "I prayed for salvation last summer. Maybe I don't get how everything works together. Karen acts like a different person. Sandy has never behaved like us. So—why hasn't my life changed? I'm still Kathy Alisson. I had hopes of a different lifestyle after Granny and I prayed while we took a walk. She says the key is to spend time with God."

Kathy shut down. She chewed the inside of her lip as she gazed across the room.

Karen's heart went out to her. Her friend was saved and she didn't know it. Kathy would never be the person she once was. The outward changes took time and active participation on her part. She should read the Bible daily to improve her relationship with God. Now Kathy could have the inner help from the Holy Spirit to change her life.

Sandy passed the fruit bowl across the table to Kathy. "Surely your granny told you Jesus never fails. He loves you too much to leave you on your own."

At first, Kathy shook her head, and then she nodded. "She did. But I expected to feel like a new version of me. Just like Karen. It was an awesome thing to watch her transformation. Look at this pajama party. The girls she invited. She still works to improve herself, and I like that."

"I feel like the same Karen, yet I'm not." She tilted her head to the side, and focused on the cupcake container on the counter. "The difference is that I believe God's promises are true. I'm learning to trust Him to keep His word. Sometimes I don't like myself. Yet I keep on the same path. I hope to become a better me."

Kathy waved both hands in the air. "Right now all I hear are a lot of words being thrown at me. Am I saved or not?"

"What do you believe?" Sandy asked. She moved around the table until she stood beside Karen. She picked up her cousin's hand, and squeezed her fingers once Karen looked up. "God reaches out to us even when we refuse to respond. Talk to Him when you're in doubt. That works for me. Remember He hears our prayers and answers each one. I guess that sometimes I don't like His answer."

"All I want is to know the God my granny loves," said Kathy. Then her lips moved without a sound as she prayed.

Karen marveled at the girl's silent prayer. Her ears perked up when a faint noise stirred upstairs. She checked the clock on the microwave. Silently sighing, she studied Kathy's bright eyes. Tears trickled down her cheeks.

"I like that happy expression. Keep it. Looks like the show must be over. I think they're about to come downstairs. Let's wash your face before they see you."

Karen pulled Kathy to her feet, and Lisa stood up and beat them to the door.

Karen grinned at her friend when Lisa touched Kathy's shoulder as they passed by.

"Kathy," Lisa said.

Although their gazes locked, Kathy turned away. She exited the room before Karen. Karen followed after her, but she sensed that Lisa trailed behind them.

In the hallway, a shadow traipsed down the stairs. The girls moved swiftly to the bathroom. Once inside, Lisa sat on the tub's edge while Karen grabbed a face towel from the linen closet. She loved the simple remedy. Hot and cold compresses had kept her family from noticing that she cried sometimes. She longed to hug Kathy as she stood at the vanity with her head bowed.

Kathy took the damp cloth from Karen's fingers before their gazes met in the mirror. Her mouth opened as if to speak, and then she snapped it closed.

"You're not alone in how you feel," said Karen. She wrapped an arm around Kathy's body then peeked at Lisa through the mirror. "Here's my story. But please don't ask questions, just let me talk. I find it difficult to talk about this to anyone, but I will. Last spring my life looked hopeless. Defeat completely overtook me, and I didn't see any way out. I was in deep trouble like I'd never experienced before."

Her eyes closed as she relived the past. She laid her cheek on Kathy's shoulder. "Everything was fine when I woke up that morning. Usually I eat a bowl of cereal, but that day I got up early and cooked a fantastic breakfast. I returned to my bedroom after I ate, with less than an hour to get ready for the community center. I needed to dress quickly.

"One moment I brushed my hair with thoughts about the last day of school. But in a split-second I burst into tears and couldn't stop crying. In less than five minutes my life became impossible to live."

She supported her head on the towel rack. This was something she'd only told Sandy. Although these girls were close friends, some family problems must remain private. She needed to be honest without sharing too much.

"That day was significant for many reasons. It was impossible for me to function at all. For the first time, since I joined the class three years ago, I missed my drama lesson. I lay in bed all day with the covers pulled over my head. I refused to talk to anyone. Mom sat beside the bed and tried to reason with me. She failed. I simply couldn't concentrate on anything she said. Her words sounded like gibberish. Hopelessness consumed me. I couldn't even move."

Oh Lord, this is hard. I feel like I'm being pulled into a trap. Should I share something this personal?

"Afterwards, I discovered she'd wanted to take me to the hospital, but Dad wouldn't agree to seek outside help. I'm glad he opposed what Mom wanted to do. Doctors probably would've given me medication that I didn't need. Even though my parents disagreed on what to do to help me, my family showered love on me that day. Jason kept coming into the room to rub my head. Brenda relieved Mom and sat beside my bed. Yet I couldn't respond when they reached out to me. To make matters worse, I left the house when everyone left my bedroom."

She shuddered at the memory. The pain jarred as much as it had when she lived through the episode last May.

"Just before dark I realized everything in the house was quiet. No one had checked on me for about ten minutes. At once the room shut in around me, and I had to escape. I walked out the front door without a destination in mind. Later I was told several people had called the house. I'd been spotted in every section of town while I wandered around the city alone. I guess I walked around in circles until I stopped in front of Sandy's house."

Karen watched her friends' inquisitive gazes in the mirror. She was happy their expressions revealed concern and not contempt. They seemed to understand the serious experience she'd undergone. The solidarity in the room encouraged her.

"I didn't ring the doorbell, but I stood on the sidewalk, and stared through their front window. Once I decided to go inside, my aunt appeared on the porch before I reached the steps. Aunt Fran ushered me into the house while she called off the search party. It was eleven o'clock by then. The entire Duncan and

Wilson families searched for me. Even my grandparents scouted around the town."

Unable to sit still any longer, Lisa joined Kathy and Karen at the vanity. "Why didn't you call me?"

"Call us," said Kathy. "I would've dropped everything too."

"There was no other way to get through it but by myself. It was like being in a daze after the initial breakdown that morning. Everything else that happened was very blurry. Mom was livid and terrified when she and Dad got there. She was ready to take me to the hospital. But Aunt Fran convinced her to let me spend the night."

She smiled even though she felt like crying. "Kathy, I'm telling you this story to encourage you. I had already surrendered my life to Jesus the month before it happened. Umm, you see, I felt like you do now. The same, as if nothing had changed. I counseled with Pastor Scott after services that Sunday. He talked to me for four hours, then he fed me dinner at Burger Barn. He's a kind man. He and his fiancée took me to dinner every day that week. She'd gone through a similar breakdown and was a tremendous help. I like the way they work together. They've known each other forever. I hope I meet a man willing to work with me."

"Butch Hayes," her friends said at the same time.

The smile on Karen's lips reached her eyes. "Spiritual growth takes time. We do the work of God by believing in the One He sent. Jesus. Hang in there. We'll get stronger and better. Each day we wake up to a new beginning. Another chance to build on a firm foundation."

Lisa brushed tears from her eyelids. "This is unbelievable. I'm shocked you didn't run into any of your friends while you were out there. I still don't understand why you didn't call us. We would've come over and stayed with you. Me, Kathy, and Joann.

You know Joann would've put everything aside and come with us. What happened to set you off?"

"I was completely stressed out. Too many problems that I couldn't control weighed me down. My parents and friends couldn't help me. Nobody could help me." *No—body—else—could—help—me.* "Only God. I'm glad He did. The rest is history, you guys. I'm still standing."

She turned around to hug her friend. "Oh, Lisa, don't cry. I'll cry too if I keep talking this way. This time is for Kathy and not for me. I've accepted what happened and I moved on. Don't worry, friend. It'll never happen again."

She ran hot water over the towel, and handed the wet cloth back to Kathy. "I love your granny. She makes me feel welcome whenever I visit your house. I wish my grandparents in Chicago lived with us."

Lisa leaned her chin on Karen's shoulder. "Did you switch topics on purpose, or can I ask questions?"

"On purpose. I want to forget everything about that day except that I came to my senses. Perhaps tomorrow."

"This is a bombshell. I want to understand what happened to you, now."

Karen shook her head. "I can't. It's difficult to tell another person's story."

"That means you're not the only person involved. I thought as much. I'll understand if you can't reveal anything more than you already have. I love you, best friend."

Kathy spun around, and faced them. "I love you too. Group hug."

Chapter Fourteen

Angela polished her toenails and whispered to Sandy when Linda walked into the room. She'd come down earlier but the family room was empty. She'd thought they were in the kitchen and she ran back upstairs. Still unable to settle down anywhere, she tried to make another connection.

Uncertainty spoiled the splashy entrance she'd expected to make. Deflated, she looked around the room. Where were Karen, Kathy, and Lisa? No one was in the kitchen. She'd checked there first. Linda had sat at the table when she found the room empty. Her thoughts filled with what to do, once she reached the family room. She resisted the pull to push herself forward. Linda wanted to be asked to join in. So she waited for Sandy and Angela to notice she stood there.

Angela gazed her way and smiled. "Welcome back. We were discussing the basketball team's pregame tonight. Hope we won."

"Most of my friends were there," Linda said.

She settled onto the floor next to Sandy and twisted her bare feet in the air while she studied her toes. Her mind sought ways to redirect the conversation to her desired topic. Why waste time making small talk when urgent issues needed to be discussed. If what she wanted to happen did happen, she could forget Joann's and Kathy's opinions.

Linda grinned when Sandy tossed a popcorn kernel into the

air. She caught it with her mouth. *Leave it to her to do the unexpected. Sandy refused to fit into anybody's mold.* On second thought, Linda was pleased that the other girls were gone. She was nervous about her mission. The topic she wanted to discuss had seemed more urgent upstairs than it did now.

"Where are the other girls hiding? I heard noise when I came downstairs. No one was in the kitchen."

"Maybe they're changing into their pajamas in the guest bedroom," Sandy said. "That's what Angie and I did before we came in here. Put on your pajamas. You can change in either the bathroom or the bedroom."

"I will in a few. What have you all been doing?"

"Well, we have some good news," said Sandy. "Kathy gave her life to Jesus."

This slumber party sounded like a "come to Jesus" moment. How did Karen decide which girls to invite to this party? She shut out two friends to ask two girls she had only talked to on occasion. Was the scheme Karen's idea, or were these two in on the plot?

That's okay. I can play their game and win.

She steadied her voice when she spoke. "Oh, I see. Divide and conquer can be a winning strategy, or so I hear."

"It was Joann's idea to watch television, and the rest of you joined her," said Angela. "Besides, we don't operate that way. Do we, Sandy?"

Sandy laughed. "Get them any way you can. In this case the end justified the means."

"Stop joking," Angela said while she joined in the laughter. "I tell Sandy that if she keeps on teasing people someone might think she's serious."

Sandy set the empty bowl aside. "Not Linda. She knows Kathy grew up with a Christian grandmother inside the house. Those seeds were planted a long time ago. For the record, Kathy gave her life to God before tonight."

"Really? Guess she forgot to inform her alter ego of the change. She's still acts like the same Kathy I've always known. But forget about that. I want to talk to you and Angie before everyone else comes back."

Angela slid closer. "The floor is yours. What do you want to discuss? We'll try to help if we can."

"Watching *Parallel Words* was a waste of time for me. Nothing sunk in. I was too busy thinking about our discussion before going upstairs." Linda squirmed on the floor to get comfortable.

She inched forward. "Here's the first question. How do you handle gamesters who aren't bad people?"

She waited, pleased with herself for finding the perfect topic to start it off. Maybe the conversation will shift to where she wanted it to go.

"Gamesters?" asked Sandy. "Do they enjoy playing games, having fun? Or playing games with, or on, other people. Which one?"

"The latter one," said Linda. She wished Sandy would move on.

Angela and Sandy glanced at one another.

"That question is way too general," Angela said. "We need more information. Elaborate a little. Give us something to work with."

"Okay, I'll fill you in on what happened when we got here. Lisa and Evette argued before we got comfortable. Now I feel guilty because I figured Lisa would snub Evette tonight, but I didn't warn Evette."

"Wait, how could you warn Evette unless Lisa preplanned an attack that you knew about? That didn't happen, right? Because if she did, why would you bring Evette?"

"It just happened. They immediately went after each other. You had to be here. It was almost like a trip to the movies."

"Well it's good you stayed quiet. It's unwise to raise an alarm on a hunch. I think it was better not to interfere in case you were wrong."

"But I figured Lisa might slight Evette if possible. She's very good at using bullying tactics to get her way."

"Lisa was at fault? I'm surprised. She normally doesn't go after people without a cause. What made you think she would target Evette?"

Shocked, Linda munched on a potato chip before replying. "Are you kidding? Lisa is relentless. Once you're on her radar screen, she refuses to let up even an inch."

Sandy knitted her brows together. "Be fair. Evette isn't on Lisa's radar. Who attacked first, Lisa or Evette? Oh, wait, that's right. Evette rode over with you this evening."

"Now I'm really confused." said Angela. "Why would Linda bringing Evette tick off Lisa?"

"It didn't. She's after Diane, not Evette," said Linda. "Lisa's upset because Diane and Karen are real close. She hates competing unless she wins. So far, she hasn't."

Angela stood up to stretch. She covered her mouth with her hands when she yawned. "Wow! So, how does that idea connect with Evette? What's the question? I feel like you're walking me through a maze."

"I can't believe you still don't get it. Lisa's working on the jealousy angle. I'm the pawn. I hate being used. Should I have brought Evette tonight knowing the facts?"

Angela traded glances with Sandy again. "I still don't get where you're going with any of this. You're talking in riddles and assuming an awful lot, girl."

"I'll help you," said Sandy. "Linda thinks that Lisa is using her to make Karen jealous. She talks to her more at school, and things like that. That makes Evette in the way because Linda brought her here." She laughed when Angela shook her head again.

"I'm trying to get this. Okay. Did Evette overreact to something Lisa said?"

"She did, *but* I'm simply tired of playing games with everyone. I want a peaceful night without drama."

Angela replaced the top on the nail polish. "Did you mention your suspicions about Lisa to Karen before coming? She knows her friend better than we do. But I'm curious. Why did you come and bring Evette?"

"Duh, I was invited just like you. What are you getting at?"

"The reason you came to the party. Are you saying that being invited mattered more than protecting the girl you brought with you? Evette would've stayed at home if she didn't expect to enjoy herself."

Don't you dare turn the table on me. I should've asked the question I wanted to discuss the most. These two are making me even angrier than I was. It's time to squash this useless conversation and begin a new one.

Linda searched for a generic answer that would completely end the discussion. "Karen's mostly cool again. She and Kathy have always been less obnoxious than their buddies." She grinned at Sandy. "Your cousin has acted like a prima donna since seventh grade. But she's behaving more reasonably these days."

Sandy's gaze pinpointed Linda. "We all picked up bad habits in middle school. Some of us learned how to manipulate others for personal gain. From what you've said, I'm surprised you showed up at all."

"Your cousin invited me, okay? I've known her since kindergarten. What about you? You and Karen can't seem to get enough of one another. Even in elementary school you went everywhere together. Can't you ever go anyplace without the other one tagging along?"

Sandy looked like she wanted to laugh. "We do it daily. But I'll level with you. Growing up was harder on Karen than it was on me. She busted her tail trying to make her friends accept me. It took a while for them to learn we were a package deal. If they wanted her to go to parties or hang out with them, they had to include me. In time they discovered no Sandy, no Karen. My aunt wouldn't allow Karen to go anywhere I wasn't invited."

"Whoa. I just thought you wanted to be a part of the group." Linda laughed at the eyebrow Sandy raised. "You knew certain unnamed individuals laughed at you behind your back? You showed up anyway so Karen could go?"

"Behind my back? They laughed in front of my face. I'm seldom clueless about people disliking me. However, I'm not a saint. Karen and I always help each other. She has done plenty of things for me. We're friends as well as cousins."

Linda switched her gaze to Angela. "Sandy answered my question, so I'll answer yours. I came to bring Evette."

"No—no. You brought Evette because you came," said Sandy. "You could've asked her to hang out with your friends tonight. I don't know your reason for coming. But you should know."

That's the problem. I don't know why I came or why I believe the things I believe. It boils down to what is right versus what is wrong. I'm frustrated. Joann and Kathy and possibly Karen and Lisa have a different mindset from mine on an important issue. What else do we disagree on?

Linda appreciated that the rest of their crowd wasn't invited. Regardless of how Karen had made the final selections, she asked the best of her friends to come. She racked her brain to answer Sandy's question, and settled on the obvious response. "I came because your cousin invited me. She and her friends are so popular that everyone likes them, even juniors and seniors. Well, at least the ones whose opinions count."

She sat up straight, studying the girls. "Don't pretend not to know that you and your friends are popular, too."

"I never thought of myself as being popular," said Angela. "I like my friends, and my friends like me. Maybe Jeff is popular, but I'm not. We all have flaws and secret hurts. No one gets a pass."

"Not even members of the dream club?" Linda shot back. Her gaze lowered to the floor.

Karen and Sandy had always had one another. Neither of them had ever had to search for friends.

"I don't think either of you understands how it feels to be an outsider. Sandy is more reserved than Karen is. Having a built-in friend has advantages. You too, Angie. Somehow, having older brothers and sisters makes life easier."

Linda withdrew before she finished speaking. An urge to cut her losses quickly set in. Leaving early seemed to be the only solution. Why should she beat herself up and stay until morning? She closed her eyes to remove the fog from her brain.

"Will both of you admit that you're popular now and have always been a part of the in crowd?"

Laughter caused Sandy eyes to sparkle. "It's a church thing. That's where I met all my popular friends."

"People call us popular. Imagine that," said Angela as she mulled over the idea.

The room became quiet until Linda's voice broke the stillness. "I have one more question to ask. This one subject tripped me up during our earlier discussion. I can't concentrate on anything else but this."

She hesitated when alarm appeared on Angela's face. Alert, her body tensed at the girl's reaction. But Linda was determined to know how Jeff and Angela made their relationship work. Not many couples graduated from high school still in love after dating for four years.

Sandy picked up crumbs off the floor. "If it's bothering you to that extent, let's hear it."

"Bear with me while I clear up my fuzzy thinking. Okay—I revealed too much about my private life before going upstairs. I feel like I was being judged for my beliefs. Everyone looked down on me. The group made me feel awkward about my views on having sex outside of marriage. It was like being put on notice that my beliefs are wrong. We should be able to have discussions without finger-pointing."

Surprised, Sandy blinked at Linda. "I can't speak for Diane and Evette, but everyone else in that discussion practices abstinence. Some of us do have friends who disagree with our values. That reality keeps us from acting judgmental about our beliefs. The scripture basis to avoid sex outside of marriage seals the deal for me."

"That's my stance as well," said Angela. "Most of my friends express their beliefs on every subject discussed in the mainstream. Social media rules with most of them. They speak out against hate crimes, drug usage, and any topic out there. Yet, those same girls discuss their sexual escapades as if that was okay."

A sadness overtook Linda as she listened. Her thoughts were still scrambled. She needed to go somewhere by herself to think. She rose clumsily to her feet, and wished the door could meet her halfway.

"Using drugs is illegal, and so is committing hate crimes." Linda edged toward the door. "I'll be back."

She hurried from the room and rushed into the bathroom down the hall. She wanted to hide somewhere where no one could judge her. Once inside, her gaze locked onto the mosaic tile. Linda turned to the door when someone knocked.

Chapter Fifteen

Sandy slipped inside the bathroom once Linda opened the door. She leaned her back on the shower, and wondered what to say.

Nothing comes to mind. I'm lost. Why did I follow her?

She resisted the urge to leave, and strode close to Linda.

"What's wrong? Don't deny that you're very upset. Something clearly isn't okay. You're not yourself tonight." When Linda turned away, Sandy moved around to stand in front of her. "Even though we've never been best friends, we've always stayed connected. Talk to me."

Linda starred intensely at Sandy until their gazes finally met. "Your cousin didn't stay connected."

"We are in a bathroom in Karen's house. Don't change the subject. I won't go unless you ask me to leave."

Tears glistened in Linda's eyes. "What if I have a lot to say?" She visibly tensed as if she expected to hear a negative reply.

Sandy sat on the tub's edge and waved her hand as if she brushed Linda's comment aside. "We're at an all-nighter. We both have plenty of time to say whatever we want to say."

Linda launched into speech with a strained giggle that caught in her throat.

When she hung her head, Sandy sat on the floor beside her at a loss for what to say next. However, one fact was very clear. She had missed the chance to help someone she truly liked. Liking Linda meant she should've opened the door that Karen had closed.

It's too late for a redo, but I can do better after this.

Linda pressed her hands against her chest. "Talking to you and Angela gave me enough information to make a decision. But I shouldn't have unloaded my problems on you."

"Why not? Believe me, I would dump my problems onto you in a heartbeat if I thought it would help. Earlier, finding out we had a different viewpoint about sex outside of marriage than yours threw you off track."

"Plus my own second thoughts made me feel used. I refuse to fall into the same trap as the one I fell into in eighth grade. Whether my decisions are good or bad, they have to be my own."

Good. You realize you've made an error. Now you can make better choices.

"I agree. Stop beating yourself up. The past is dead. Bury it. Let it go."

Linda rested her head on her palm. "It isn't that easy. I made two of the biggest mistakes of my life."

You made a mistake. Don't make it worse by feeling sorry for yourself. Then it really will be hard to break the cycle.

"Join the club. Who hasn't slipped up? You can change the present and the future, but not the past. Stop worrying about your mistakes. Just make better decisions now."

Linda fiddled with a drawer pull. She opened and closed the drawer repeatedly. "I don't believe sex outside of marriage is wrong. It was just wrong to sleep with those particular boys."

Hmm. I guess being halfway right is better than being completely wrong.

"Sandy, the people you choose as friends matters. But walking away from the girls I hang out with is terrible. It's like parking the car we're riding in and leaving my friends stranded. Trust me. Being rejected doesn't feel good."

"You don't have to reject them, reject their ideas. But, like you said, the people you hang around with matters. You will make the hard choices. See? I already have faith in you. What are you thinking about?"

"Karen's friends. Everyone wants to be like them, despite their stupid ways."

Sandy laughed. "Really? Who told you that lie? I don't, and neither do you."

"How could Karen, Kathy, Lisa, and Joann choose those girls over me? No matter which way I look at what happened to us, their pushing me away still doesn't make sense."

"I know. It boggles the mind. What else is bothering you?"

"My mom. We haven't discussed the having sex issue in-depth. Other than her telling me not to do it because I may get pregnant. Her old-fashioned views annoyed me then, but now I'm angry. She harped on unwanted pregnancies while withholding birth control protection that would've kept me from getting pregnant."

"You've been having unprotected sex? Why? I'm sure your mother wasn't against birth control. She probably didn't want you to sleep with the boys you dated."

"Then why didn't she make that point? Instead, she spoke in a hidden code that only she understood. Kathy and her mother talk about everything."

"To deny you birth control is the same as saying 'I don't want you to have sex.' You chose to misunderstand what she meant. Talk to your mother about the problem tomorrow. Don't allow the birth control issue to ruin the relationship with your mom."

Linda dabbed her face with a paper towel. "I will. With luck, she won't tell my father. Sometimes we share secrets with each other. Maybe tomorrow will be one of those times."

"None of us has a perfect relationship with our parents. Not even Kathy, but hers is close. I don't know about Diane and Evette. Even when I disagree with my parents, I'm willing to hear them out. They know more about life than I do. Which is the problem I have with Chris. He's one of the few people I like and my parents dislike."

"What about Cody Kennedy? You know he likes you. He tells everyone that he does. He even told Chris."

Sandy pulled the lace on her pajama top, and almost ripped it off.

Is that why Chris asked me if Cody had asked me out?

"Hmm. He told Chris that? It's news to me. I started dating Chris before Cody broke up with his girlfriend."

"What does that matter if Cody is the right guy?"

Sandy grinned. "If I break up with Chris, he might be an option to consider."

Linda stood up when Sandy did. "How are you able to date Chris if your parents don't like him?"

"Chris can visit me at home on weekends, but I can't go to many places with him. When I do get to go, my father drops me off and picks me up. Since school started, we've only gone out three times. I see him more at school than anywhere else."

She hugged Linda. "I've been in your business long enough. Come back to the party when you're ready."

She left Linda staring at her face in the mirror.

Sandy replayed the conversation to herself on the way to the family room. Karen dangled Cody in front of her all the time and only tolerated Chris because of Sandy.

* * *

Kathy opened the bedroom door. "I'm hungry. Let's eat some fruit before we go back to family room."

The girls had changed into their pajamas and waited for Lisa to step into her slippers.

Lisa joined Kathy at the door. "I'm having a munch attack. Watermelon sounds good, but any fruit will do. Hope there's some fruit leftover."

The girls left the guest bedroom and headed to the kitchen. Lisa grabbed a watermelon wedge from a bowl inside the cooler. Kathy went straight to the counter. She ate grapes until the dessert container caught her eye. She selected a cupcake, removed the milk carton from the refrigerator, and poured herself a glassful. Karen set a plate filled with diced apples on the table.

She did a cupcake count. There were only eighteen of the delicious treats left. Diane probably should've baked two dozen more cupcakes.

She waited for Kathy to sit at the table. "Give me the scoop on you and Joey. You two are becoming tighter. I can tell."

Kathy winked at Karen after she peeled off the cupcake wrapper. "Yeah ... sort of, kind of. We're moving in the same direction, and it feels good. I want my time with Joey to last forever."

"I'm wavering about my boyfriend," said Lisa. "Half of me wants to boot Kevin. The other half says don't be hasty, you may need him. What do you all think?"

Kathy rubbed her hands together. "Finally, I get to weigh in on my favorite subject. Date more guys than him. Sweeten the pot. Don't ignore the boys who run after you. Let them catch up."

"Truthfully, I don't want to date anyone for a *long* time. I just want to go out with my friends. Two weeks ago, I started taking piano lessons again. I want to play well. To practice as I should will take up most of my free time."

"Don't look at me," said Karen. "You already know what I think.

They say that opposites attract each other. But you've got to have more in common than you look good together."

"I agree with Karen. You and Kevin are like the east and the west. You two will never meet up."

"We might," said Lisa, laughing.

"Nope." Kathy spoke through a mouth filled with cupcake. She drank milk to wash it down. "Polar opposites don't stand a chance."

"Yeah, well, you and Joey balance out each other perfectly. He's aloof and you're outgoing."

"She's right," said Karen. "His serious attitude complements your whimsical nature."

Kathy's eyes lit up. "Whimsical, huh? I like that characterization of me."

"Using words with more than ten letters is disgusting," said Lisa. "So don't do it again."

Karen poked Kathy with her finger. "Do you know what's odd about your and Joey's relationship? You're an extrovert that loves privacy, while Joey's an introvert who opens up to his friends."

"That's because other people are more interesting than I am. I'd rather talk about everyone else." She grinned at Karen. "*Lisa, are you going to drop Kevin? His personality fits in with Joann more than it does with yours.*"

"Ah, but a relationship between the Ice Princess and King Kevin won't work," said Karen. "Their egos compete for dominance whenever they share the same space."

Lisa laughed. "Be nice. Don't be a hater. Or, are you upset because Joann watched that deplorable show in your bedroom?"

"Deplorable," said Karen. She counted each letter on her finger. "Ten letters. Okay, you made it, but barely. Be careful, people might find out you're smarter than they are."

Lisa blew an air kiss through her lips. "Shh, don't blow my

cover." She turned to Kathy as she grabbed a napkin. "Why did Joann choose Ice Princess for her nickname?"

Kathy answered while they cleaned up the mess they'd made. The girls left the kitchen, and headed to the family room, but they stopped to wait on the shadow that came down the staircase.

Diane jumped off the last two steps, and ran up to them. "Hi guys. Did you miss me?"

"Of course we did," said Kathy.

Diane giggled as she grabbed Kathy's arm and held on tightly.

Karen beamed at the animated girl. "Glad you found your way back to us. How was the show?"

"I hated it. I should've stayed downstairs with you guys." Then she launched into a lengthy explanation of why the program was awful.

Kathy burst into laughter at Diane's report of *Parallel Worlds*. Her scathing critique was very funny.

Karen paused at the doorway to the family room. She had thought Linda was still upstairs. But Linda sat cross-legged on the floor, as she talked to Sandy and Angela. Now only Joann and Evette were left inside her bedroom. She noticed that almost all the girls wore pajamas now. Of the ones downstairs, only Linda and Diane still wore clothes.

When they entered the room everyone grabbed a floor pillow and reclined beside the other girls. No one jockeyed to sit next to a certain person. Instead, each girl talked with the person who sat next to her.

Only Diane scurried across the room away from the group. She knelt on the floor in front of boxes stacked up against the wall. After choosing a game to play, Diane read the instructions out loud and then looked up.

"Time for a board game. Karen play *This Versus That* with me."

Lisa flopped onto her stomach. "May the rest of us play? Or was the invitation only for Karen?"

Diane scanned the instructions again. "The directions say up to six players." Her gaze fleeted from face to face. "Does anyone else want to play?"

"Yes," said everyone except Linda.

"Not me," she said. "The show's been over for an hour. What are they doing upstairs? I expected you all to come down right after I did." She looked at the other girls. "Forget about Joann's opinion. The show wasn't that great. I zoned out before it ended."

"Look at Karen's face," said Diane. "She warned us not to waste our time and energy. Next time, I'll listen." She unpacked the game in the empty space beside the girls. "I left them watching a comedy video. Evette insisted and Joann agreed. It was funny, though, based on Christian stuff." She gazed at Linda. "Sure you don't want to play?"

"Ugh," said Lisa, "do you know how to count, missy? Only six people can play. Linda makes seven."

Karen shook her head at their foolish jibes at one another. Lisa attacked Diane, and Diane goaded Lisa. *I've never noticed Diane provoking Lisa before tonight.* She stifled a groan at the expression on Kathy's face. Trust her to level the playing field wherever possible. To favor the underdog was good unless you selected the wrong person to defend. So far Lisa had behaved well since the original gaffe. Diane battling Lisa might prompt Kathy to butt in.

Chapter Sixteen

Kathy squinted at Lisa. "I counted to ten before meddling, but I had to say something. Do you remember saying, 'I'll never be the same,' less than thirty minutes ago?"

"Lisa Douglas! You believe Jesus died and rose again for your sins?" asked Sandy. She reached across Angela and patted Lisa's back. "That's great! He's the only way to the Father. How does it feel to be all in?"

Lisa sat up, chuckling. "That comment brought out the cheerleader in you fast. But I'm insulted. You sounded amazed. I didn't make a formal declaration like Kathy did. I've always known about Jesus. What person doesn't know?"

"Plenty, and they live in the U.S. with us. Most people have heard the story and know His name. Only they don't believe that the event truly happened," Angela said.

Karen decided to give Lisa a way out. "Guess what! After seven months of begging her, Lisa is going to the youth meeting with me Wednesday. We'll walk over together if the weather is warmer that day. I refuse to walk in cold weather to any place other than school."

Diane discarded the board game before the setup was completed. She crawled across the floor, and squeezed in between Sandy and Karen. "What all did I miss when I watched that dumb show?"

"Loads of stuff," said Angela. "We discussed everything from our boyfriends to growing up in Shiatown. The highlight came when Kathy recommitted her life to God."

Lisa chuckled. "Now that was something I didn't see coming. I'm not normally a skeptic, but time will tell. We'll see."

The glacial expression gave the warning. Kathy was prepared to fight.

Did she forget about blasting Lisa five minutes earlier?

"Oh, don't stop now," she said. "Finish the thought. See what?"

Lisa spread out her fingers and peered at her nails. "What else? Will you do the Karen thing and reinvent yourself? A new attitude will make life better for anyone who knows you."

Although Kathy pointed to Lisa, she focused her glance on everyone else. "There you have a typical Lisa comment that makes no sense. Shut. Up. Who are you to judge me?"

The silence that followed revealed everyone's private thoughts.

That comeback was way too personal. Neither girl had ever gone that far before.

Karen sought Kathy's eye, but Kathy refused to look at Karen. Lisa wouldn't look at her either.

Okay, I'll direct this discussion for both of you. Do not take it off track again.

"Going to the youth meetings has helped me in a lot of ways. I'm learning how to live out my beliefs in God. I don't do it well *yet*. The folks in my trig class saw me shoot down the know-it-all who sits behind me. But I'm getting better. At least, I hope I am."

"Nice try," Kathy whispered into Karen's ear. "It's payback time for Lisa. No problems. I'll be gentle. Shush, Karen."

Lisa rotated her shoulders. She studied Kathy's face the entire time she did so. "I heard the word 'shush', what else did you say?

Oh, we're not talking now?" She lowered her voice to a loud whisper. "Too bad."

"Youth meeting," Diane said. "You've invited me before. The problem is that I can't leave the house if my parents aren't at home. They're always gone on Wednesdays. I'll try to find a way to come this time."

Sandy's lips curved into a smile. Her eyes lit up too. "I hope so. I want to see you there."

"I've always wanted to go with Karen. I'll probably join the chorale group instead of the drama team." Diane twisted her lip between her finger and thumb. "Somehow I have to pull it off. It won't be easy."

She flashed Karen a smile. "My folks might agree if you come home with me after school. My house is closer to the church than your house is. That will be wonderful if it's cold outside. I'll pay you back for my meal tonight and cook us dinner."

Her gaze followed Karen's gaze to Lisa. "Lisa's invited to come over too. We'll all walk to church together."

The sigh Lisa gave sounded more like a moan. "You never stop trying, do you? No need to answer. You don't and you won't."

Confusion appeared on Diane's face as she stretched out her hand to Lisa. "I don't know what you're talking about. Help me out."

Lisa sat up. "I said you would mess up again, and you have."

Karen snapped her fingers. "Forget eating at either Lisa's or Diane's house. I have the perfect plan. If we eat dinner here, I'll convince my mom to cook seafood." She rubbed a hand across her stomach. "Her hushpuppies are irresistible. We'll pick up Kathy on the way to church, unless she wants to eat dinner with us. Do you?" she asked the grinning girl who nodded.

Karen brushed her hands together. She was enthused that Kathy did her part to de-escalate the problem.

"Perfect. Kathy agrees. Now how does that suggestion work for everyone?"

"Perfect? For who? Not for me," said Lisa. "Nothing's changed since I woke up this morning. I still hate for other people to plan my day."

"Ooh, she's pouting. Look at those droopy lips."

Lisa rose slowly to her feet. "Hush, Kathy. Now, isn't hush a softer word than shut up? Your helping Karen to smooth everything over doesn't count when you snipe at me. I'm tired of your drivel." She swung around to Karen. "Your alternate plan didn't work. I'm hungry. Let's eat some fruit in the kitchen. *Please.*"

Karen raced to the door without an answer. She was delighted she didn't have to drag Lisa out of the room. "Bet I beat you," she said, and dashed into the hallway. She removed the fruit bowl from the cooler while she waited for Lisa to join her.

"I don't like that girl," Lisa said when she entered the room. "This last flare up is her fault. She enjoys making conflict between you and me. She's a peace disturber."

Karen set two foam plates on the table along with a bowl filled with grapes.

"Don't say that. Something is *way* off here. You've known Diane since sixth grade. She's not herself tonight."

Lisa filled her plate with grapes then sat at the table. She popped a grape into her mouth. "What makes you think I'm talking about her?"

Karen held a grape between her fingers. "Because you are. You and Kathy argue all the time."

Lisa laughed. "So, I dislike them both."

"I won't buy into your distractions. This is about Diane, so admit it. You have to go back into the family room and finish out the night without a fight."

"So say you." Lisa popped another grape into her mouth. Her

eyes took on a happy glow. "*Diane Meredith.* You have to admit the name has a certain pizzazz."

"Don't waste our time. I expect this night to end without another fight. You know how to lay low."

"Humph. What's with this fixation on Diane? Why blame me if she isn't herself tonight?"

"Please, be serious. Diane is not only my friend, but she's also a guest inside my home. I would never behave this way at your house."

Sadness entered Lisa's eyes. She looked hurt. "Stop trying to make me feel guilty. It's *her* problem if she's off-kilter. She needs to stand down. I've been nice to that girl, and she still won't quit."

"Uh-uh, you've treated Diane better than usual, but not nice. There's a gigantic cleft between the two. You know that." Karen pushed her plate aside. "Try harder to mend the fence you personally tore down. Forget about tonight. You've tormented Diane too many times in the past. Now make it right."

Lisa picked up her plate and looked around the room. "Time to put the food away. Let's clean up the kitchen and get back to the party."

"Not until you promise to overlook what happened in the family room with Diane *and* with Kathy."

"Kathy went *way* over the top this time."

"So did you." Karen dropped her plate into the trash can. She stood on her tiptoes to remove enough bowls from the pantry to store the leftover food. "Joann, Kathy, you, and me need to talk about our friendship. We act more like enemies than friends."

Lisa laughed. "Not you and me. Diane called Kathy and me frenemies. I like that word."

"I don't." Karen pounded her fist on the counter. "I'm tired of the old act."

"Sick of our friends who aren't here? Join the club. What did

I ever see in those girls? I'm glad you didn't invite any of them to the party. Sometimes Kathy makes me angry, but I would do anything for her."

"That's how I feel about Joann. She would treat me better if it wasn't for you."

"That's out of my control." Lisa removed a broom from the pantry. "Let's switch the subject. I'm sick of Kevin. Drop him into the pot of people to avoid."

"You always say that he's history, so ditch him."

After she put on gloves, Karen took sanitizing wipes from a container. She needed physical activity to settle down.

Too much is going on, even for me.

* * *

Inside the family room, Linda's gaze was glued to Diane. Something was off. Her behavior seemed peculiar. Diane resembled a child who'd been abandoned away from home. She fidgeted as if she couldn't relax.

Linda kept watch.

Her eyes are narrowed and she nodded her head. Did her lips move? Is she talking to herself? Yes, she is. Just like she was sitting in the room alone.

Linda disliked where she figured Diane's thoughts were headed. She squashed her anger.

I hope Diane doesn't confirm my suspicions.

But Diane appeared restless as she gazed into the hallway. She seemed eager to leave the room. She glanced at the other girls. "Guys, I could eat something else before I go to bed."

That's it. Overkill. Diane's possessiveness of Karen had pushed Linda to the limit.

"Leave Karen alone. She might persuade Lisa to go to the

youth meeting with her. Eat later. I'll keep you company in the kitchen when you go."

None of the girls spoke. Everyone waited for Diane's next move.

She seemed to consider Linda's suggestion until stubbornness won out over fair play.

Diane scowled at Linda. "Lisa's choice to stay at home means she doesn't want to go. Don't claim anything different."

"You can't criticize me when you're clearly wrong. You are not hungry. Stop the lies. Forget the schemes. Your best effort won't break up Lisa's and Karen's friendship. Too many other girls have tried and failed."

"Mind your own business! Talk about something you know about. Karen has lots of friends. I know other people too."

At first Linda hesitated, and then she laughed. "Aw, but she's not your best friend, is she? Why? Because she's Lisa's best friend. Now deal with that."

Before Diane replied, shadows across the room captured Linda's attention. Evette strolled through the doorway while Joann followed close behind.

"I heard that comment," Joann said. She sat on the floor next to Angela. "It's okay for Diane and Karen to hang out together. My goodness, they're friends. Plus, they have more in common than Lisa and Karen do."

It felt like a starburst ruptured inside of Linda's head. All the oxygen left the room. Escape became her heart's desire. She might lose her sanity if she stayed longer.

That's it! I've taken enough of Joann's junk tonight. Something about that girl really irks me.

"You all are pathetic and the biggest bunch of insecure babies I've ever seen." She pointed her finger at Joann. "You just got here. How can you know what's going on? I'm sick of you and your uninformed opinions. Next time, listen before you speak."

The other girls' accusing gaze failed to move Linda. Even Joann's awkward expression left her cold. "You guys act like kids. My little sisters don't behave as silly as you all do. Diane wants to tag along to the youth meeting with Karen and Lisa. So Lisa refuses to go. Since they're together in the kitchen, Diane wants to eat."

The incredulous expression on Joann's face frustrated Linda even more.

She doesn't get it. Stupidity might be a part of her DNA.

Then smugness entered Joann's expression. She pointed to herself. "It's my fault that Diane is jealous of Lisa?"

"No. It's your fault that you're jealous of Karen."

Linda clasped her hands when the 'I get it' light failed to register on Joann's face.

She's priceless. I could overlook the silliness if she was truly dim-witted. The Ice Princess is too stuck on herself to care about anyone else.

Linda slapped her hands on her thighs. "I give up. If Diane charges into the kitchen, Lisa will leave the room." She patted the floor in front of her. "Then, you get to sit next to Lisa. Big deal. Grow up!"

The alarmed expression on Evette's face made her pause. Linda's kitten displayed the same bewildered expression whenever visitors came over to visit.

Evette's a newbie. She looks like a trapped animal seeking freedom. Good idea. It's time to go home.

Evette touched Linda's shoulder when she sighed to calm herself.

"It'll be all right," she said into Linda's ear. "I finally get why we were invited. Karen's wants to bring us all together."

That was Karen's plan. But it was too late for reasonable thoughts at this point.

Linda had reached that place of no return. She'd invested too much energy into her fury to change her mind. She would lose whether she stayed at Karen's or went home. She preferred to feel bad in private. Linda wanted to sulk alone. Too bad going home branded her a loser in the game they'd all been playing.

"I'm through," she said, and struggled hard to truly mean it.

Had she anticipated too much in coming this evening? What had she expected to happen? Who knew? Linda didn't. She probably never would know. Remorse hit her when Evette squirmed on the floor. Evette looked distressed and Linda wanted to stay. Yet it was too late to back down. She would look like an idiot if she did. Her mind made up, she fled the room, and hurried to the kitchen. Linda tilted her head on the door, and watched the friends who cleaned up the room together.

Karen loaded silverware into the dishwasher then smiled up at her. Lisa waved to her as she wiped off the counter. The scene broke Linda's heart. The best friends had a grand time while the hostess's party fell apart.

Chapter Seventeen

Linda looked depressed. Something was drastically wrong. Karen stalled for time until she dropped the last fork into the container. Out of things to do, she shut the dishwasher, and backed up against it.

"Hungry?" she asked. She hoped to hear a simple yes.

Linda slumped on her feet as if her strength had seeped away. The girl who liked straight talk appeared uncertain. Linda bluffed her way through every trial she faced. She talked a good game but was sensitive to how other people felt about themselves and how they felt about her.

What happened? I've never seen her out of control before. She's upset, not angry. Sandy's not intervening means it must have been explosive. How can I lighten the mood?

"What's wrong? Please tell me nothing."

Karen's heart turned over when Linda batted her eyelids to keep from crying. She went straight to Linda and hugged her. Lisa drew near and laid her head on Linda's shoulder.

Her retreat to the kitchen with Lisa hadn't stopped the blow up in the family room. The expression on Lisa's face said it all.

Karen prayed for a restart. "Talk to me. Say whatever you want to say and I'll listen."

Linda refused to meet her eyes. "I can't. But it isn't your fault. I'll be able to explain myself much better tomorrow."

Linda couldn't go home. She was one of the main reasons Karen had decided to have a pajama party. It was an attempt to undo the wrong she'd done. She'd cast the wrong people out of her life in seventh grade.

"I treated you awful at Jefferson Middle. I'm surprised you even speak to me."

The tears that flowed from Linda's eyes caused Karen to cry too.

"You're at my house for the first time in four years. I finally understand how important your friendship is to me. This pajama party is for you. Please stay. Give me another chance to make things right between us."

Linda wiped her eyes with the napkins Lisa handed to her. "I can't. I just can't." She tossed the used napkins into the trash can and accepted some more from Lisa.

Karen grabbed on to Linda's hands. "You called my house a safe zone when you accepted the invitation. We won't rebuild our relationship if you go home. You'll never trust me again."

Regardless of the upside of Linda's staying, Karen struggled to plead her case. Too many years had passed since she'd shunned the girl she should've embraced.

"Please stay. I don't want you to go home. Give us another chance."

Lisa touched Linda's shoulder. "We promise not to aggravate you if you stay. I'll be nice to everyone for the rest of the night."

Linda glanced at her. "Is that a promise you can keep?"

"I'll give it my best shot. You know I try to keep my word whenever I give it out."

Karen forced herself to smile. "You know that's an honest answer. What do you say? Will you stay at the party with us?"

"Um, no—I can't. I'll call you later this weekend. I promise."

When Linda sped from the room, she collided with Evette and Kathy, who rushed to the kitchen.

Evette yelled as the girls grabbed each other to keep from falling.

Linda placed a hand on her chest. "Are you all okay? I'm glad no one was hurt. I didn't hear you coming."

Linda sped away. She darted into the family room, and snatched up her belongings, while she casted everyone else's things aside. Still crouched on the floor, she turned to Angela. "Will you take Evette home in the morning?"

Angela studied the baffled girl who hovered in the doorway. "I will, but it won't be necessary. Evette plans to go with you. I want you both to stay at the party. Don't go away angry."

"I'm fed up, not angry. At least, not anymore. I think I'm just tired."

She stood up and frowned at everyone. "Friends warned me not to come tonight. I should have listened to them. No offense to you, Karen. You offered friendship, and I accept it. I think you know what I mean."

She sighed when Karen nodded. "But, I'm sick of your friends. All of them."

With her belongings in her hands, Linda bolted out the door. Although she swiftly left the room, she appeared strangely reluctant to leave.

Angela rose and scurried out behind her. The girls heard her call to Linda as she walked down the hallway.

* * *

Karen covered her face with her hands for a second. She made eye contact with her cousin. She was halfway out the door when she spoke. "Oh boy, I can't believe any of this happened. I'll be right back."

The girl chewing popcorn nodded at the silent command. Years ago, experience taught Sandy to expect the storm before the quiet could prevail. She brushed crumbs off her lap, and waited to see what occurred next.

Evette quickly placed her backpack onto her shoulders, and grabbed her pillow and blankets. "Goodbye. I'll see you all at school Monday." She hurried her steps, yet hesitated in the doorway as if she didn't want to go. After Evette whispered to Kathy, she scampered off behind Karen and Lisa.

"I'll be right back," said Kathy. She returned minutes later and stood in the doorway. "Oh no ... I just saw Karen's mother and sister on the stairs. Maybe we were much louder than I'd thought." She left again, but immediately returned, and poked her head inside the door. "Linda and everyone are still inside the house. Maybe they won't go home."

She hurried away but came back quickly. This time, she walked into the family room. "Everyone is still in the foyer. Karen's mother and sister sat on the steps. I agree with Karen. I can't believe any of this happened, either. We were all on the right track too. Well, at least for awhile. But now we have the full picture. Lisa creates scenes and Linda directs them. She's a pro at setting the mood."

"Stop poking fun," said Sandy. She rubbed her neck and shoulder muscles with her hand. "This situation is serious. Or was that your nervous response to what just happened? Either way, you should have kept those last comments to yourself."

Joann turned her eyes away as she reached for the discarded bowl of potato chips. "Don't go thoughtful on us. Admit that Linda acted like a wild woman. I walked through the door and got jumped."

"Don't forget you were gabbing when you hit the room." Diane maneuvered onto her knees. "Like Linda said, you spouted out opinions without the facts. But of course, that's typically what you do. Vintage Joann, right?"

Joann's lips relaxed into a smile, only her eyes were dim. "Ooh, forgive me for defending you. Next time, girl, you're on your own."

Diane studied Joann. "Defending me? Is that what you call it? You love to put yourself first. Good thing I don't depend on you. You own this flop."

Joann leaned on her elbows. "Excuse me? Well look at Miss Feisty. The little nobody who hopes to belong. Win any friends lately?"

Diane gasped as if she'd taken a punch to the stomach. She stared at Joann with her bottom lip nipped between her teeth. Her eyes filled with unshed tears.

Sandy finally understood why they sniped at each other. Diane was in survivor mode while Joann was too stubborn to admit she was wrong. Still, Joann's heart was nowhere near as rebellious as her mouth was. All night Karen ran herself ragged to hold everyone's hands. Perhaps it was best to let the flames die out on their own.

It took me a while to understand what's going on. But now that I do, I hope everyone else will join me.

Pleased with her inaction, Sandy rolled onto her belly. She rested her chin on steepled hands.

It didn't take long before Diane resumed the dialogue where it had ended. "Simply brilliant. That was a classic Joann remark. No, I won't excuse the way you knock Karen. I won't excuse how you always throw Karen and me together." She dried her eyes with her fingers. "You should stop. Those antics won't make Lisa like you more than she likes Karen."

Joann parted her lips to speak, but she glanced at Kathy who winked at her. "Huh. I don't push you and Karen together. She deserves better than you. A smart girl would lose the attitude before her one friend becomes history. Look, Karen's busy reinventing herself. She likes you. Don't ruin the relationship by your implosion."

Sandy silently applauded Joann's peace offering despite that it came with a hit. It was Diane's turn to forgive Joann and accept it. She wanted to rummage through the attic for Brenda's sleeping bag. Sandy disliked babysitting girls older than herself. This pajama party was indeed a godsend, though. Some people would label the party as being chaotic; it wasn't. Healing was taking place.

"Diane," said Sandy, "I like to hear you speak up for yourself. However, a few of your remarks stung. I know, confrontation can get messy. It often does." She faced the other combatant. "Joann, cut Diane some slack. We all deserve a break from the drama."

Kathy fanned herself with her hands. "I agree with Sandy. I'm exhausted. You all have worn me out tonight." She giggled once Sandy squinted at her. "Okay, I played a tiny part in the arguments."

Sandy nudged Kathy with her elbow. "Linda and Evette left the party. I confess, the blowup caught me off guard. I acted clueless and just let it happen."

Joann removed the top from a bottle of water. "Yeah, well, what did you expect us to do?"

"We can act normal and lose the drama. Playtime is over. Why can't we get along for once?"

"Be more like you? Treat people well who don't deserve my respect? I'm not selfless. It's all about me. I have sharing issues."

"Joann—you're too giving to have sharing issues. You just want everyone else to think you do. Also, you know the right thing to do even when you refuse to do it."

"Like straightening out this horrid mess we created? Agreed.

What else can we do?" Her gaze darted to the girl who hadn't spoken in five minutes. "I don't have anything against you. I just want you to know that."

Startled, Diane gave her a half smile, and then she turned away to wipe her eyes.

Kathy jumped to her feet and danced a jig across the floor. "I'm ecstatic! We just had two major showdowns that didn't involve me." She grinned at Sandy. "Are you proud of me or what?"

Sandy slid a tissue box across the floor to Diane. She shook her head when Kathy dance around the room some more. The girl was genuinely happy. She couldn't contain her smiles.

"Let's hope the discussion outside goes better than the one in here. Or are they still inside the house? A conversation in the foyer might mean that Linda and Evette decided to stay until morning."

Chapter Eighteen

Although it was freezing outside, Karen wanted to move the conversation onto the front porch. She hated that the girls were huddled in the foyer. Her mother and sister sat on the top step. They'd listened to every word so far. Annette stared at her. She probably thought about what had happened to Karen last May.

Stop worrying about me, Mom. I'm fine. That will never happen to me again.

Too bad the noise inside the family room had disrupted the entire household. Nevertheless, she could handle the situation without their help. At least her father remained upstairs inside his bedroom fast asleep. Unless he hid out of sight and secretly watched what happened too.

My mother will step in if we don't patch up this trouble soon. Only God knows what she'll say.

Karen squinted at Angela when the girl swayed on her feet. Either Angela kept beat with an inner tune, or she was exhausted. She pleaded with Linda and Evette not to leave earlier than they should.

"Linda," Angela said in a persuasive voice, "I still think the conversation we had with Sandy bothers you more than this latest episode."

Linda opened her mouth to answer, but glanced at Annette,

who sat in the shadows next to Brenda. They sat close enough to hear every word and to see each girl's facial expression.

"Sandy made a good point," she said. "I don't even know why I showed up to this party. I only accepted Karen's invitation because we used to be friends. So here I am, miserable and going home."

Karen's shoulder sagged under the unhappy admission. This was the last thing she wanted to hear. That her sleepover was an utter failure. The old friend she'd planned to win back hated that she'd come. At one time, the two girls had been very close. That is, until the gang absorbed all of Karen's time. She invited Linda to win back her friendship. So much for redeeming herself to the friend she hated to lose.

"Did Sandy question why you came to Karen's sleepover?" Lisa asked. "Why? That's crazy. We've known each other since kindergarten."

"Crazy, huh? How about you being friendly with me to spite Karen? Admit you tried to make Karen jealous. You can't handle that she likes someone who's not in your precious group. She likes Diane, so get over yourself."

Lisa's gaze swept the stairs before she blurted out an answer. She stuck her hands into her pajama pockets. "Why do you believe I'm being friendly with you to aggravate Karen? We've known each other since forever."

"You answered your own question. Listen to what you just said. I've seen this act since kindergarten." Linda laughed then shook her head. "Your group is a joke, by the way. I can't believe you call those pitiful girls friends. Only the four of you here tonight are worth talking to. The rest of the gang is pathetic."

"We've always gotten along well together. What can I say? Some girls are friendlier than others."

Linda's mouth hung open before she gathered her thoughts.

"That's your defense for why you dropped me for girls too stuck on themselves to have a clue? Sure, they're popular, but just wait until the people who admire them grow up and they don't."

The girls stood in silence until Lisa held out her hand, palm up. "Straight talk. I'm not jealous of Diane. I dislike anyone who tries to break up my friendship with Karen. They can hang out together without her pulling Karen away from me. As for you and me, I enjoyed it when we watched our sisters' basketball game together. Don't forget, I sat beside you. *I* suggested we shop afterwards and eat at Burger Barn. I suggested and you agreed. That proves we still have plenty of things in common."

"You, Karen, Kathy, and Joann dropped me as a friend in seventh grade," Linda said through clenched teeth.

Lisa clasped her fingers together then moved closer to Linda. "I can only speak for myself, and I didn't. Who knows why we stopped being friends."

"I do. You never wanted another friend besides Karen."

Lisa eyed the stairs again. Sighing, she faced Linda. "That's ridiculous. Karen isn't my only friend. Let's start over. I'm happy you're here."

"You left me out," Evette said. "Are you happy Karen invited Linda? Or are you happy that Karen invited me and Linda?"

Mischief entered Lisa's expression when she chuckled. She tapped a finger on her lip. "Let's see, how does that witty little saying go? Oh, yeah. If the bed belongs to you, lie in it. If not, don't be defensive. Did I get that right? That's not a nice thing to say to anyone, is it?"

Karen touched Evette's arm. "That was Lisa's way of saying, she's glad you're here. I invited the girls I wanted to hang out with tonight. Thanks. I'm glad that you came. Everything is working out well."

Evette's eyes opened even wider. "How can you say that when

Linda and I are about to go home? Do you still believe that God told you to bring us all together? That's strange talk and I go to church every Sunday."

"Oh, I told you about that, huh? The faces of everyone here tonight popped into my head while I prayed. I thought the Holy Spirit led me about which people to invite. Especially since the faces were of the girls I wanted to come anyway."

"Thanks for your honesty," said Angela. "It's hard to reveal personal beliefs and experiences, but you did. You're right. God does direct our paths whenever we let Him." She appeared unsure until she grasped Linda's hand. She refused to let go. "Please stay. Help us iron out this mess we made. I think Evette wants to eat breakfast with us." She whispered into Linda's ear. "Nothing will be accomplished if you leave early. Don't go."

Linda's expression revealed that she was unable to reach a decision. Although the inner struggle held her captive, the wishful gaze exposed how she felt. Linda wanted to stick it out. Finally, she smiled at Angela and studied Evette. "How about it? Do you want to stay or leave? I'll stay if you agree."

Karen beamed at her mother. Patience worked every time. You just had to hammer those little obstacles into submission until they finally disappeared. *See Mom, you didn't have to step in to help us after all. Ooh, I love happy endings.* She wrapped her arms around her body in a congratulatory hug until she noticed that Evette remained silent.

Evette stared at a picture that hung inside the dining room. She appeared to be mesmerized by the Duncans' family portrait. She eyed Karen. "At school today, two girls confronted you outside the office. They were angry because you didn't invite them to your party." She ignored Lisa when Lisa asked her who the girls were. "They were hateful to you. Yet you faced them, and you never backed down. Why did you choose me over one of them?"

Lisa tapped Karen on the shoulder. "Who tried to box you in? No one questioned me about your guest list."

"Although it did hurt a little, I'm over it now. I didn't want any of them to come, and they're not here. So there. I'm happy with the outcome."

"They should've left you alone. Only a fool will badger you to come where they weren't wanted. We'll talk later."

"Most of your friends are flighty," Evette said. "Since you only invited three girls out of that crowd, I'm glad you chose Kathy, Joann, and Lisa."

"Wow!" said Lisa. "Did I hear that right? Did you just validate me?"

Evette turned to Lisa. "Yeah, I guess so. Even though I disagree with a lot of the things that you say and do, you're usually not rude. They are. This may get back to the group, but I don't care. They act ridiculous. Who do they think they are?"

"No, it won't. That will never happen," Karen said. "What is said here, stays here. No one else will ever know what we've discussed at my house except for the people who are here."

"Yeah," Lisa said in a low voice. "Thanks for including me as part of the real-deal bunch." She touched the astonished girl's arm. "I'll tell Joann and Kathy about what you said later. That'll make them happy."

"Good idea," said Angela. "We'll tell the other girls what we discussed, and find out what they talked about while we were gone." She urged Linda down the hallway, and beckoned to the other girls to follow.

But Evette hung back. She refused to speak, and stared at Lisa until Lisa moved farther away. When Evette still refused to talk, Lisa finally rounded the corner and disappeared.

Once Lisa was gone, Evette returned her attention to the portrait. "My family doesn't have a family portrait. Individual school photos of us kids are all we have. You all look natural. Like you belong together." Evette eyed Karen with curiosity. "Do you like me or am I just your latest project. Uh-huh," she said when Karen gasped. "Last year it was Diane. Is it my turn?"

Filled with remorse that she hadn't sought Evette out sooner, Karen hugged her. "I've offered you friendship all year. That means I like you."

Evette returned the hug. Mist filled her eyes when she pulled back. Her eyes were red like she'd been crying.

Karen knew this was a special moment never to be forgotten. Even if they never became close friends, Evette wanted to spend the night. Had they jumped the final hurdle with this latest flare-up? If so, the healing could truly begin.

Arms entwined, the girls ignored the two women huddled on the steps. They re-entered the family room as they walked side by side.

Once there, Karen separated herself from Evette, and returned to the doorway. She wanted to linger and see firsthand what had developed from the talks, both inside and outside the family room, but more pressing dialogue was in the cards for her. Karen resigned herself to what she had to do. She cleared her throat to gain their attention. Everyone looked at her.

She gave a slight wave. "I'll be back."

She left the room and moved swiftly until she reached the foyer and gazed up the staircase. Her mother waited for her on the upstairs landing.

"Your bedroom?"

Chapter Nineteen

Annette shook her head. "No, we can talk here. I won't keep you longer than necessary. How are you?"

"Fine, Mom. Really. Things are going great."

"Great? Then tell me why two guests were going home before morning?"

Karen scaled the stairs in record time. She settled on the top step to keep an eye on the traffic in the hallway. Her gaze raked over her sister. "How much did you all hear?"

Brenda leaned onto the banister. "Not much. Just enough to understand that something was seriously wrong. The raised voices and the general chaos made it seem like things were out of hand. The atmosphere had that charged, something-is-about-to-explode vibe."

Annette touched Karen's shoulder. "I'm waiting. Bring me up to speed."

"Oh, Mom. It's been a long night. Linda and Diane got into a battle of words." She grinned when Annette's eyebrow rose. "Sooo ... Linda decided to leave, and Evette chose to go with her."

She blew air through her lips. The sound reminded her of a whistle blowing. "I won't fool myself, or you. It's been touch and go all evening. Only a few of us wanted to get along. As far as consideration for each other's feelings? Forget it. For some of the girls it wasn't on the agenda."

Karen rose and stood beside Annette. "I really believe things will be better going forward. I'm not just saying that to keep you inside your bedroom."

Annette's eyes sparkled like diamonds. She looked like she wanted to laugh. "Is 'battle of words' synonymous with 'heated argument' these days?" She smiled when her daughter nodded. "Did you talk to Diane? Is she willing to forgive and forget as Linda is?"

"I didn't have time to talk to her, but why wouldn't she be?"

"Let's hope that she is. Tell me why some of the girls watched television in your bedroom? There's a TV in the family room."

The tension that had eased hit Karen full force. How did her mother know about that? "It's Joann's fault. She demanded to look at a paranormal series she likes to watch. Most of us didn't want to see it, but she was in the mood to have her way."

Annette brushed her finger on Karen's cheek. "Listen to me. You said this sleepover would bring old friends back together with a sprinkling of the new. Here's the rule of thumb as you go forward. Tell the girls if you don't want them to do what they're asking. Remember why you asked to have this pajama party. Who knows when you'll have another all-nighter."

"Ooh, that doesn't sound good." She backed down when Annette's eyes narrowed. "Okay ... will do. I promise not to let you down anymore."

"You didn't let me down this time. I understand your expectations. Your dad and I are proud of you."

He's proud of me. After the way I've treated him. She can't be serious.

Still, Karen was relieved. She'd expected Annette to drill her longer than she had. Plus, her mom hadn't mentioned the conversation in the foyer. Linda and Evette had criticized the missing girls' behavior. Her mother had let that entire conversation go.

Of Karen's gang at school, her mother liked Lisa, Kathy, and Joann the best. Annette limited Karen's activities with the rest of the group. That's why Karen seldom invited those girls to her home. She'd reduced her outings with them to sports events at school on Saturday afternoons. So far, the girls didn't suspect that she'd limited her time with them. Only Kathy had noticed the sleight, and she had commented on it before tonight. Nope, the girls in question had no idea Karen avoided them whenever possible.

Happy to get off so easily, she hugged Annette, while giving Brenda a thumbs up. "See you in the morning." She kissed her mother's cheek then checked her watch. "Hmm, maybe I should say in the afternoon."

Annette held Karen at arm's length. "Looking forward to it. We'll discuss the conversation in the foyer after your guests leave."

Ooh, I won't get off free after all. We're doomed to have the 'how to choose your friends' discussion. She'll expect an explanation for Linda's and Evette's comments about the rest of the gang. My life will truly be different after we talk. Oh, Mom!

Annette stared at her daughter. "Look at me. I accept your word that you're not anxious or depressed about what happened."

"I'm tired but not depressed. I don't understand what happened to me last May. But trust me that I'm being proactive this time. I refuse to keep my feelings bottled up inside." She backed down a step, as she held onto the banister. "I'd better go back downstairs. I don't want anyone to look for me."

Brenda slapped her on the back when Karen lingered. "Hang in there, champ. You're in the last play of the ninth inning. Your navigating between third base and home. Scot-free, until tomorrow."

Karen raced down the steps. "Your comment doesn't help."

She breezed into the family room and slid into an empty spot beside Sandy.

The low-key atmosphere excited her. It was proof that the girls attempted to get along with one another. Had the spirit of what Karen hoped to accomplish finally sunk in? The contention had toned down considerably.

Everything appeared to go well on every front. Linda's and Evette's belongings were back in the space against the wall. Her cousin and Diane chatted together. Both girls appeared equally invested in the discussion. Across the room, Evette and Joann engaged in a conversation.

Delighted, her gaze centered on Kathy and Lisa who played cards. From the looks of things, the girls talked more than they concentrated on the game. Only Angela and Linda were missing from the room. Evidently, they continued their earlier discussion somewhere else in private. Even though no one's faces teemed with joy, they all appeared settled in for the night. Karen had much to be thankful for. Particularly since the party was about to come to an end.

I think we're close to a breakthrough. Thank God for another chance to set things right. No more starting over. I'm on my way. At last.

Diane smiled at Karen, but she continued to talk to Sandy. "Do you think Angela will take me home in the morning? I walked over here after school with Karen."

Sandy nodded. "She'll pass by your house on her way home. Will it be too early for your folks to pick you up? My parents sleep in on Saturdays and so do Karen's folks."

"Normally, my parents do too. They went out of town for the weekend. I have to find my own way home."

"Really?" Sandy tapped Karen's shoulder with the back of

head. "Did you know Diane thought she had to walk home in the morning?"

"No, I did not know that. She's a secret keeper."

"I am not. Don't say that, even if you're joking. Next you might begin to believe it yourself."

"Karen is a tease," said Sandy. "So am I. Seriously, her sister would've taken you home if you'd asked her."

Diane looked confused. "Oh—Brenda said she likes to sleep in on Saturdays. She's staying up late to write a term paper. I didn't think she would get up early to take me home."

"Why not?" asked Karen. "Taking you home is more important than Brenda getting her beauty sleep. Speak up next time."

"I haven't stayed alone in my house overnight," Sandy said. "Someone is always there besides me. I spend the night with Karen if everyone else is out of town together. Who'll be at home with you tomorrow and Sunday?"

"Myself. I'm used to staying in the house alone." She turned away from the surprised look on Sandy's face. "I enjoy being by myself. My folks are usually at home on weekends. I'm mostly at home alone during the week."

"Excuse me," Sandy said when she yawned. "Karen's sleeping over at my house Saturday night. Come over and join us." She checked the clock on a three-tiered shelf. "I mean, tonight. I like to have the people I like around me."

Obviously pleased by the comment, Diane mulled over the offer. She shifted to her knees, and looked at Karen, who nodded at her. "Karen agrees. First I have to tackle my parents. Once I come home, I'm stuck in the house if one of them isn't there." She quickly explained once everyone looked at her. "My father doesn't want people to see me go in and out of the house alone."

"Stay here. I'll pick you and Karen up at four. We're eating dinner at Burger Barn before we go to a movie. My brother will play taxi driver for us. We're on our own once he takes us home after the movies. Chris and crew will drop by at eight to play games. After that they're going to a party I can't go to." She covered her mouth when she yawned again. "My parents will drop you off at home after dinner on Sunday."

While Diane and Sandy discussed their plans, Karen studied Evette. She had turned around when Chris's name was mentioned. Was it her imagination, or did Evette scoot a little bit closer to listen?

Why does her reaction to that boy's name bother me? Either something's up with Evette, or with Evette and Chris, or I'm delusional. But I think I'm pretty sane right now.

In her peripheral vision, she saw Diane bounce up and down.

"Karen, pay attention. We just finalized our plans for tomorrow and you weren't listening." She repeated the previous conversation, and then she waited for Karen's reaction.

Karen liked the idea. "Sounds like a winner to me. I'm all in with the plan."

Even if I must put up with Skip and Trey—and with Chris, when I think about it.

Chris and his friends used to occupy her gray area. The situation was like the one described in her cousin's poem. Once Chris began to date Sandy, Karen placed the boys under a microscope, and she hated what she saw. Decepticons! They were deceitful in ways that she couldn't explain. At least not well enough to describe what she saw to Sandy. Had anyone else seen their sneaky side? Maybe she should take a vote and see.

Karen paid attention when Diane laid her face on Karen's shoulder.

"I'll call my mother in the morning, but she'll put me on speakerphone," Diane said. "I prefer to talk to my mother without my father around. She usually gives me the time I need to properly frame the question. They always say no if they cut me off before I finish the explanation. He does that all the time."

"Hopefully he won't this morning," said Karen.

She wondered about her friend's home life. For once she understood why Diane never went to the youth meetings with her. She couldn't leave the house unless one parent was at home. Karen had invited her to attend each week for seven months. That meant Diane's parents were never at home on Wednesdays.

How does she intend to go next week if they're not at home?

Diane crossed her fingers. "I'll call my mother in the morning. Hope she says yes."

"Count me in, too," said Kathy. "I'll join you all after the football game tomorrow." She laid down her hand and grinned at Lisa. "Beat you. I won. Diane, come out and watch the Tigers win this afternoon. That is, if the temperature reaches fifty and the sun is shining before one. Those are Karen's requirements to cheer her team to victory."

"I give," said Lisa after she counted up the points. "I missed whatever you all said. So much for concentrating on the game. I lost." She stood up and stretched her arms. "Okay, who's going where, and when?"

Sandy filled in the blanks. "Diane and Karen will spend the night at my house tomorrow. We'll eat dinner at Burger Barn. I don't know which movie we'll see, but we're doing that too. Kathy said she'll meet us at the restaurant after the game."

"Kathy, why are you staring at me?" asked Lisa.

A Cheshire grin broke over Kathy's face. She looked serious, until she grinned again. "No special reason. I'm just a happy person. Don't you agree?"

"No. I don't. Oh, I get it. You expect me to fuss that Sandy excluded me tomorrow."

"I did not," said Sandy. "You're always welcome at my house."

"I know. I'm stuck at home tomorrow with my relatives. But, I refuse to go to anymore of Kevin's competitions. He really ticked me off this time."

"I like that comment, good for you. I've adopted that same approach with Chris. I'm calling the shots. My mother insists on it." Sandy threw her head back when she laughed. "Back to spending the night. After the movies, Chris and his friends are coming over. Then they'll head to Steven's party."

Lisa frowned. "Skip and Trey? Think I'll pass."

Sandy looked at Karen before she turned to Lisa. "What's wrong with Skip and Trey? They seem okay to me. What do you have against them?"

Chapter Twenty

"Um, let me think about it a little," Lisa said. "Anyway, it's more of an impression than real evidence. I don't know them well enough to have an opinion. I'll sleep on it. What do you think, Karen?"

Thanks for the pass. Now I have to weigh in. This is not a conversation I want to have with Sandy.

"That I need to sleep on it myself. I'll get back to you. I prefer not to base my opinion on dislike."

"I'll think about it, too," Diane said. She studied Sandy with hero worship in her eyes. "It's wild that you can ask me to spend the night without your mother's permission. That won't happen in my house. My parents don't do company well."

Ah! Diane's folks dislike houseguests. No wonder I never made it past the living room. Diane is unhappy at home, and I was trying to improve her social life.

Insight flowed from every direction. First, Linda made the case for safe sex. Then, we discovered that Angela broke up with Jeff. Now, we know Diane spends too much time at home alone. Undecided about what to say, Karen watched as Angela and Linda strolled into the room.

Angela sprawled beside Joann. She licked pink frosting from her fingers.

Linda clapped her hands once she reached the middle of the floor. Her glossy brown eyes glanced at each girl.

"Forgive me for stomping out of here earlier. That's the kind of prima donna antics I hate the most."

Sandy paused as she brought a hand filled with popcorn to her mouth. "We know. You typically go without a word to anyone. Ten minutes later, you return to rescue the person you left behind. After that, you leave again. Sound familiar?"

Linda burst into laughter. "Seventh grade. Only, we rode our bikes over here that evening. I like to think I've matured a whole lot since those days."

"I think we've all grown up since then. Especially tonight." Sandy twiddled her fingers in her lap. "A lot of drama has happened to all of us. Some good ... and some, not so much."

"Don't jinx it. I'll fill Angela and Linda in on what we talked about," said Kathy. "Some of us are eating at Burger Barn today around four thirty. Feel free to stop by if you like."

"Count me in," said Angela. "Was this preplanned or was it a spur-of-the-moment thing?"

"Half and half," said Sandy. "Karen had planned to spend the night with me. We'd already decided to eat dinner at Burger Barn and see a movie after we ate. Diane's folks are out of town for the weekend. She'll ask her mother if she can hang out with us until Sunday. Pray that the answer is yes."

"You're at home alone for the weekend?" Angela asked. Her voice was low, almost a whisper.

Diane's sigh sounded more like a hiss. She briefly closed her eyes. "My folks are usually at home on weekends. I'm by myself Tuesday through Thursday."

Kathy grimaced. "Ooh! No wonder you're always at Karen's house. I would be too."

"I wouldn't mind if I could invite friends to spend the night,"

Joann said. "Here's a solution for you. Tell your folks you need a little more family time. My father would spring for a new wardrobe if I asked to spend more time with him and my mother."

"No way. Our arrangement works out well for us. I think we've gotten used to the setup."

"Then why do you practically live with Karen?" asked Joann. "Nope, I'm not buying your excuse. Try another one."

"Please—I don't visit Karen every day. I don't even visit her every week. This is my first time to stay overnight since sixth grade. We're friends, just like you and Karen."

"Don't get upset. You do visit Karen a lot. Are you and your mother close?" asked Kathy. "I love to pass time with my mom. She's fun. Now, my dad, so-so. Too bossy."

Diane jumped to her feet and folded her arms across her chest. "Stop asking questions about my personal life. How my family treats each other is none of your business."

Stunned, Karen stood up fast, and wrapped an arm around Diane's shoulder.

The sad gaze she gave Karen told the story. Her friend felt lost and all alone. That was the result of absentee parents and no siblings. Still, her response to Kathy was a little harsh even if it was true. Kathy had meant no harm. She hyped up family life whenever possible.

"Whoa," said Kathy. She stretched out her hand as if she warded off a blow. "I didn't mean to insult you. I tell anyone who'll listen about my family's weekends. When football season ends, my mom and I fill our Saturday afternoons together. After my tennis lessons, we get our nails and hair done, after that we pick up my granny. Granny likes to eat at The Main Street Diner. My dad uses the day to bond with my brothers while they work outside in the yard."

Her body shook when she giggled. "I think I got the better deal with my mom and my granny, don't you?"

Diane pulled on her fingers as she separated herself from Karen. "I—I apologize. I shouldn't have snapped at either of you. My comment was nasty, and that's not me. It's just that ... well ... let's just say my mother and I are not that close." Her gaze darted to all the girls. "Don't feel sorry for me. My folks are getting what they deserve. Each other. Let them spend their time together. I won't have to put up with either of them."

Diane appeared to regret the last remark. She shut down right away, rocked a little on her feet, and placed her fists beneath her chin.

Karen understood her friend's abrupt withdrawal. Like Karen, she didn't want anyone to discover her family troubles. Although Diane had exposed a lot of information, Karen was certain that none of these girls would gossip about what they'd heard.

"Do you want to talk about the problem?" Evette asked. "Talking to someone who doesn't know the other people involved can help you. That's what I do every time I miss my best friend from home. I call my cousin and cry about the friendship. We discussed everything together without fear that it might leak out to other people."

Diane shook her head and moved to the other side of the room.

Karen sat down to observe Evette better. What she said defied logic. If you missed talking to your best friend, why not call her instead of your cousin? Unless the loss of the friend was the problem. Evette had already hinted at having a lost friendship tonight. Karen wanted to hear the details about the ruined relationship. But she placed her doubts about Evette on the back burner. Now she had the opening she'd waited for all night. It was another chance to show off good ole Shiatown hospitality.

was no way to escape the truth. Diane lived inside a troubled home. Real problems plagued the girl who deserved better treatment from her parents. Her life was falling apart while Karen tried to orchestrate her social life. Numerous red flags had surfaced before tonight, but Karen had failed to pursue each one. She'd dealt with shallow issues as Diane's heart broke. Her friend was trapped alone inside a house she hated to live in.

I never imagined Diane spent most of her time alone. Why didn't she tell me? Her parents loved themselves more than they loved their daughter. Thank God they only had one child. Who knows how they would've treated their other children. No wonder she said she was lonely last year. That was when the junk all started.

Sandy's voice broke into her thoughts. "I won't give you advice. However, my pastor is great to talk to about things like this. Will you talk to him after church Sunday? We'll find a way for you to meet him, even if your mother says you can't spend the night."

Diane shook her head. "It's not on me. My folks are the ones who need the help. I won't spill my guts to a stranger. Not even if he is your pastor. It's hard enough to talk to the girls I know."

Karen tried to squash the thought that entered her mind. When that didn't work, she hummed softly to herself. Anything was better than to do what she felt she must. How could she pretend her life was perfect? Diane deserved a friend who would help her.

Why did I expect the other girls to be upfront about their lives? I never planned to reveal anything. Did I think I was the only one with serious problems? If I keep quiet, Diane will think she's all alone. Ooh, can I help her without blabbing out my family secrets? How much information is too much to tell anyone?

Her gaze swept to her cousin's calm face.

Hopefully, Sandy will break in if I go too far. Oh well, here goes nothing.

"Uh, Diane—I love Pastor Scott. He's young enough to understand how I feel, yet wise enough to give me the insight I need to make good decisions." She gave everyone a half grin. "He counseled me last spring when my parents almost split up."

Karen relaxed when no one gasped or asked questions. Maybe she could help Diane without pointing a finger at her father. *I must keep it general. Mom says to tell people only what they need to know.*

Chapter Twenty-One

"Okay," Karen said. "Where to begin. Well ... last spring, my parents' marriage sunk into crisis mode. The whole episode caught my siblings and me off guard. Both of my parents wanted to remain in the relationship. But all of the problems brought my mother back to God."

She lowered her tone, and spoke directly to Diane. "I won't give you any advice either. I understand that your parents' choices changed your life. It must have been hard to overhear what your father said that night. Let it go. Don't dwell on it. Pastor Scott says words are powerful. I still remember their arguments. At first my dad dumped his shortcomings onto my mom's lap. When Mom stood up for herself, he accepted the blame for his stupid mistakes."

"Forgive him," Evette said. "It's true that some households are better than others. But none are perfect." She leaned closer, and boxed her out from the other girls, as if to make Karen listen better. "It's my mother who disrupts the peace in our house. Eventually my dad learned not to trap himself inside the bathroom. Each time he did, she scolded him from outside the locked door. Yet they love each other very much."

Linda chuckled, and took up where Evette left off. "My mom attacks my dad and me over the airwaves, you guys. We hear about our mistakes before we get home each day. I blame her nagging on the cell phones. Maybe she gets bored during the day; who knows. Dad laughs it off, though. He tells her to blast him after he comes home."

"See. I bet each of us can tell a similar story," said Evette.

"Except the stories aren't similar to mine." Karen barely moved her lips. She avoided looking at anyone while she spoke. "It wasn't that my dad had annoying habits or did those quirky little things that drive you crazy. But all is well now. Their relationship is back on track, so how about that. Hey, I rhymed-sort of."

She leaned back onto her elbows, and watched the expression on each girl's face.

Joann looked heartbroken. She appeared to be totally affected by Karen's story. "This is all news to me. What brought your parents back together?"

Karen dabbed her eyes with a tissue. "God. No one else deserves the credit but Him. I guess the Duncans were destined to stay together. Of course, I'm making light of a situation that almost destroyed my life." She laid her face on her palm then raised her head. "For the first time, I understood my own limitations. I felt helpless until I talked to Pastor Scott. Now I realize that I have control over *my* actions. How I responded to their crisis mattered to the entire family." She turned to Diane. "Especially to my own well-being."

"You definitely were not yourself last spring," said Joann. "I kept asking you what was wrong, but you refused to confide in me. I didn't realize it was family problems. I thought you were stressed out over the guy you liked at the community center. Is it over? Are you back to normal?"

Evette shook her head. "No, she isn't. Not until she forgives her father."

Karen watched the girl who offered her opinion where it wasn't wanted. *Who made you an expert on what is best for me?*

I've held off on judging you about how you feel about my cousin's boyfriend, and you decided to advise me? I don't think so. She took a deep breath to calm herself down.

"I have, and I do. It's over. Somehow I found peace despite what happened to my family."

Angela reached over, and touched Karen's arm. "It's evident you love your mother, but you never mention your father. How do you feel about him?"

Good question. I wish I knew the answer, but I don't. It's been seven months since I found out about an affair that ended sixteen years ago. Why can't I forget that it happened?

Karen sought the proper response. "Well, I'd rather love him from a distance. Perhaps that will change one day, but for now, it's all I can do."

"That's better than how I feel about my parents," Diane said. "Perhaps I should talk to your pastor. We'll try a different day if my mother says no. I don't want to hate my parents. Even though I think they both deserve it."

Sandy's grin broadened. "You have the right spirit: the will to help yourself. Godly counsel enables us to see beyond our limitations. Your parents may never change their selfish ways. *However,* unlike some teens, you do have some stability in your life. You have a safe place to live and enough money to buy what you need. You ace your classes at school. You'll get a scholarship to college. *Also,* you have my cousin as a friend."

Her lips broke into a smile. "As for the Buchanans, we need loads of prayer. Ask Karen. She knows the lowdown on us."

"My family needs lots of prayer and I do too," Karen said. "Pastor Scott convinced me to join the youth meetings on Wednesday evenings. The setup there is wonderful. First, we have a mini church service. Then later we break up into interest-related groups. I hang out with the drama team, Sandy's in the writer's club, and Angela attends the current events group. The church has sixteen youth study classes to choose from."

"I never signed up for a class," said Evette. "I go with my mother to pick up my brothers and sisters. They love to go there, and I do my homework at home after they leave."

"I haven't seen you at Kingdom Life on a Sunday," said Karen. "Where do you sit?" She glanced at Sandy and Angela. "Have either of you seen her at church?"

Both girls shook their heads while they waited for Evette to answer.

"Our family listens to the service from the overflow room," she said. "Our pastor in Wichita is friends with Pastor Scott's parents. He recommended my father for the lead spot on the maintenance staff last summer. My family is big, so the job perks like free rent were important. My father fit right in, so we're here to stay. That's why I wanted to make friends with you all tonight."

Lightness filled her expression. "Thanks, Karen." She paused until Karen gazed at her. "I've been in Shiatown since June, and this is my first invitation to go anywhere."

The comment somewhat lifted the gloom that threatened to take Karen over. "Aw, that makes me happy. Thanks. I just got my second wind."

"I'm glad you came," said Diane. "Join the library guild at school if you like to read. We meet Tuesdays after first lunch."

Joann held up her hand. "Look, there are too many different twists in this conversation for me to digest. Please, one discussion at a time. Now Karen, you implied that love kept your parents from calling it quits."

Karen wondered if she should agree with that opinion. She braced herself for whatever Joann had to say while Joann remained silent, consumed with private thoughts. The wheels that spun inside her head didn't seem to be about the Duncan family. Her conversation proved she wondered if her own folks' relationship was truly solid.

Lisa reached for Karen's hand. "I shouldn't have to say this to you, but I will. Call me whenever you need to talk to someone. I'm always available."

Karen pulled her hand away from Lisa's grip, and gave her a hug, while she searched for the right words to say. "I trust you, Lis. We're friends for life. My spring was miserable, but my life keeps improving every day. Jesus gave me the desire to start over. I have better friendships, plus deeper relationships with the people who matter most. I made two vows on the first day of school. I promised to treat people like their life counted for a good purpose. Also, I won't take offense where none was intended. Every life should matter enough for me to forgive anyone who asks for forgiveness. I can't keep a scorecard. Sin is sin. Jesus forgives every person when they repent."

Her heart plunged to her stomach, then slid to her feet. Even the man who slept upstairs deserved her full cooperation. With no intentions to run the show, she'd played God with both of their lives. Perhaps Brenda would come around quicker if Karen gave their father a second chance.

How? I don't ever want him close to me again. He almost destroyed our family, while acting like the perfect man that he wasn't. He's a liar. But what if he had told us the truth? Over sixteen years have passed since the affair happened. Mom was pregnant with me at the time. Why don't I believe he hasn't been with anyone else? There's no proof he's had other women besides Peggy. I could be wrong. Uh-uh. No—no. What if there were other women who had never come forward? We can't trust him to tell us the truth. He's already proven he doesn't mind lying.

Karen blinked at Diane, who clearly expected a response from her.

Ugh! What did I miss this time? I've got to stay focused. Better fess up.

"My mind wandered a little. Did you ask me a question?"

"Yes, two times. I asked if you thought your pastor can help us. My life feels unmanageable to me. I've lived this way for so long that I can't imagine anything different."

"Talking to Pastor Scott can help you make good decisions even if your parents never change. You can ask him how you can make their reality work for you. The man is a great listener who prays. Talking to him proved very helpful for me. I really needed the guidance. I still do. Maybe I should make an appointment to see him."

She hesitated then smiled. "Too bad I'm a slow learner. Sometimes I pick and choose which lessons to obey. I can't do that, not if I want to grow up. I want to be a better me in every arena. By gaining wisdom, I'll be able to help other girls like me."

Linda grabbed Karen's hand and squeezed her fingers. "People say that you are cool. They got it right this time. You are cool. Thanks for inviting me to your sleepover."

Karen tried hard to enjoy the moment. "Cool, huh," she said, hoping to keep from crying. "Guess I'm moving up in the world."

"I can't wait to write an article about tonight," said Kathy. She wrote in the air with her finger. " 'Pajama Party: The Story.' You all know that this isn't the usual all-nighter. Our time together has inspired me. I want to let the student body know what happened here tonight."

A short debate erupted as the girls disagreed with Kathy's plan.

"Okay, you're a good writer," said Lisa. "How will you frame the article without releasing details? Don't forget—What is said here, stays here."

"Trust me to make it happen without revealing any facts. Karen was on target with this pajama party. I plan to highlight the results. We broke through many real *and* imagined walls."

"She's right," said Angela. "Those little hiccups we don't think are important can be very serious."

Karen thought about her father. "I agree."

Her mind stayed on him until she noticed her cousin squinted at her. Sandy's face wore that inflexible expression that Karen hated to see. *Oh, boy, what is she up to? Something is coming that I'm sure to dislike.*

Sandy shuffled to her feet. "Tonight was fun. Lots of good changes found us by accident. Let's focus on one goal. We can tie up the loose ends on everything we've discussed, for the rest of the night. But not before Karen finds the pink sleeping bag for me." She pointed to the door. "Come on, girl, get moving. I'm ready to say goodnight."

Sandy walked out of the room without a backward look.

Karen stalled for time. She picked up empty snack bowls then set them on the table.

"When are you four going to change into your pajamas?" she asked the girls who'd watched the TV show in her bedroom. "Change in the guest bedroom downstairs. Take a shower if you want," she called over her shoulder. "Be back in a jiffy."

Out of things to do, Karen left the room. She dreaded what her cousin had in mind.

Sandy waited for her in the foyer. She gripped Karen's hand and led them to the stairs.

"It's showdown time. No rebuttals. Let me speak without interruption. I know," she said when Karen snatched her hand away. "Great ideas make me bossy. Now here's the plan. Follow your heart. Go to your parents' bedroom. Tell Uncle Sam how much you love him. Aunt Nettie already knows how you feel about her."

"What! No way. It's in the middle of the night. It can wait until morning."

"You're ready now. Tomorrow you'll change your mind and dig in."

Karen thought over the request as teardrops slid down her cheeks. She glanced over her shoulder, hoping no one overheard their conversation. "Upstairs," she said, and rushed up the steps.

The girls moved nonstop until they reached her bedroom. Karen hurried inside and closed the door once her cousin followed her into the room. She just stood there as Sandy watched her, unable to walk any further.

"You expect too much. I can't spit out words I don't feel."

Sandy removed clothes from a chair and sat down. "Consider the full picture before you disagree. You love Uncle Sam. Not admitting that love is tearing your family apart. It's time to give yourself, him, and the rest of your family a break."

"Oh, really." She placed her hands on her hips. "He didn't give us a break. Anyway, this isn't about me or the rest of the family. It's about the man who broke faith *with us*."

Sandy shook her head. "No, he didn't. He broke faith with his wife and the fallout hit the children. My dad agrees with Uncle Clyde that your father told the truth. There were no other women." She grabbed Karen's hand when Karen turned away. "Okay, at first he lied. Can you imagine making the worst mistake of your life, thinking you're home free, and then, without warning, sixteen years later, your wife discovers you had an affair with her best friend?" She dropped Karen's hand and leaned back in the chair. "Your father deserves a second chance. Give it to him."

Karen picked up a honey bear. "Why? We never received the

first chance to have a decent husband and father. What if he's still fooling around on Mom?"

Sandy swiveled in the chair. "You want a guarantee that Uncle Sam is being faithful to Aunt Nettie. Yet we both know it's impossible for him to prove his innocence. Did he learn his lesson after he made the first mistake? I hope he did. But there's no way to prove that he didn't. Not unless another woman comes forward. If one doesn't, we'll never know for sure."

Karen felt her cousin's gaze follow her as she wandered around the room. "Psst. Exactly. I refuse to live in limbo with him. What if he lied?"

"What if he told the truth? Be honest. It's wrong to punish a person for a crime they might've committed. Aunt Nettie isn't the most forgiving person, but she forgave your father."

Astonished, Karen spread out her hands. "Big deal. She's married to him. Brenda thinks he's still fooling around."

"Right now her opinion doesn't count. I'm talking to you. Brenda is reasoning out of her hurt and anger. The pain is responding for her. If not, she would've forgiven her father when he asked to be forgiven."

"Stuff that idea. For too many years he pressed both of his thumbs down on Brenda. Uh-uh. He never let up. Brenda never gave him a reason to question her behavior. She has a right to be mad at him."

"But she doesn't have the right to not forgive him, and neither do you."

Karen mashed her lips together, as she considered what Sandy said. "Uh-uh. So in your opinion we should act like nothing happened. To just forget he's a deceiver who treated me poorly, too."

"Uncle Sam isn't perfect. But he is a good husband *and* a good father. Yes, he was strict with his children. He still is. Yet neither one of you complained until you found out he'd cheated on your mother. Be rational." She paused as if she attempted to press home her point. "To hate your father for a mistake he made before you were born is wrong. You would need to forgive him whether it happened last year or yesterday."

Tears pooled in Karen's eyes but they didn't spill over. "I have forgiven him. I wouldn't speak to him if I hadn't."

"You love him and he loves you. Forgive him."

"Stop it. You sound like Evette."

She picked up the other honey bear and hugged both of them in her arms. It was late. All she wanted to do was to go to bed. She turned around and faced her cousin. "What if there was another woman back then besides the filth that left town?"

Chapter Twenty-Two

Kindness entered Sandy's eyes. "You do realize that you also have to forgive her, right? Think about this. You wanted to date before your sixteenth birthday. Now that you can, you won't. It's all because of these issues with your dad. Nice guys have asked you out. You rejected them all. You know Kathy will contact Butch. Give him a chance to win you over."

"Too late. I think I've always wanted Butch. What's the real problem? I feel like we're playing word games. Let me win so we can go back to the party."

Sandy looked defeated as she rested her head on her palm. "I'm thinking about my cousin, and you should too. You can't move on with your life without forgiving Uncle Sam. Come on, you know good intentions aren't enough to make a difference. How many times has granny told us that?"

"Brenda—"

"Has to work through her own issues with your father." She crossed the room to stand in front of Karen. "Your sister will benefit from seeing you do the right thing. So do it. You're ready. You know you are. You'll make Aunt Nettie happy. Jason forgave his dad."

Karen retreated to the window. "Big deal. He's fourteen. The two of them have always been close."

"Wouldn't that make Uncle Sam's fall from grace harder for him to accept? He's a momma's boy who idolized his father."

Karen stared into the darkness to think of what to say. She'd reached the tipping point in the relationship with her father. At first, she ignored him because it made her feel as if she helped her mom. Then she longed to watch him eat every accusation he'd flung at her and Brenda. The punishments she threw at him no longer satisfied her. Karen wanted him to leave the house. Not to divorce her mom. She wanted him to live outside of her radar. It was a juvenile assumption that she could have one without the other.

"Let's talk about Jason." She moved away from the window and lingered in the middle of the floor. "He's a headache most of the time."

"What does Jason have to do with anything?"

"He's a part of this family."

"Okay, so let's talk about him. When did he first become obnoxious? Last spring? Oh, imagine that. You're wasting time. Say yes so we can rejoin the party. I'm sleepy. It's past time to go to bed."

Karen leaned her head on the wall. "I guess he failed to escape the fallout after all. Jason had been okay until last spring. Up until then, he'd been the perfect younger brother." She squeezed the honey bears in her arms. "Ugh! I know. I should get over myself." She attempted to smile. "Only ... I've worked so hard to have my own way."

Sandy giggled. "Yeah, you did. I sat in a ringside seat for the show." She wriggled her fingers into the air. "Don't you just love these growth spurts? My mom says we grow in character when we learn something new. I had an epic battle with my mother last Friday. I grew a fourth of an inch over the weekend."

"Stop making me laugh. I bet you had another showdown about Chris. Can we talk about him instead?"

Sandy shook her head. "Not today."

"Why not? Oh well. I guess I am wasting time."

She discarded the stuffed animals and clasped Sandy's hand. "Knocking on their bedroom door will be the hardest task I've ever faced. It can wait until tomorrow. My head will be clearer in the morning."

"Um—no. Talk to your father before you change your mind. Get it over with and move on."

Karen looked for a way to say no. "Wait! I never agreed to talk to him at all. That was just your suggestion. Okay, okay, I need to buck up." She cringed. "Ooh, now I sound like him."

Sandy burst into laughter. "Yeah, you do. If you wait any longer you'll begin to look like him, too."

"Ew." Karen stumbled to the door. "Can't chance that turnabout. Let's go."

She headed down the hallway, but she grabbed Sandy's arm when her cousin veered toward the stairs. "Forget that. You're holding my hand the entire time. Come on," she said, and pulled Sandy behind her.

The girls sped pass Brenda's bedroom, but froze once the door swung open.

Her sister studied their faces from the doorway before she snapped off the ceiling light. "You're making way too much noise for people sneaking down the hallway."

"Point taken. Sorry we woke you up," said Karen. "Shoo. Go back to bed."

Brenda closed the bedroom door behind her. "I'd rather follow after you two. What's up?"

"You. So go to bed. Please! I need a private word with Mom

and Dad." She lowered her voice. "Stop staring at me. Go back to your room."

Brenda's eyes glittered in the dim lighting. She glanced at Sandy, who pointed to Brenda's bedroom. She tugged on her cousin's finger before she hooked her arm. "A private word? Fine. I'll take Sandy with me. Fill us in on the conversation later."

"Brenda ... Don't you have a paper to write?"

She dropped her cousin's arm. "Forget it. Those teary eyes make me want to tagalong. You have guests downstairs. This chat with me is a waste of time. I'm coming with you."

Karen stomped away, while she mumbled under her breath. "How do I get myself into these impossible situations?"

To talk to Dad in front of Brenda will make me nervous. She might think I deserted her. Okay—I defected. Only the why is becoming fuzzy now that she butted in.

Karen knocked twice and Sam opened the double doors. He belted the robe around him, while Annette slid off the bed, then moved closer to the trio. Her father glanced at his wife, as he ushered the girls inside the room, and closed the doors behind them.

When no one spoke Sandy finally broke the silence. "Hi, Uncle Sam. Aunt Nettie. I know it's late. Sorry to intrude."

"Hello, Sandy," Sam said. "Knock on this door whenever you like. You're always welcome."

"It's very late," said Sandy. "Thank you for being nice about it."

Sam's gaze probed his youngest daughter. "Are the girls still fighting? Annette thought everyone had settled down for the night."

Even though he spoke to Karen, he watched Brenda. Sam acknowledged his daughter whenever possible. But Brenda shut him down each time he tried. He did that same thing with Karen.

He tried to engage her in conversations he thought she might want to share with him.

I blow you off every time you try to win me over, yet you never gave up on me. If only you hadn't hurt Mom.

Karen sank her toes into the carpet. She didn't know what to say or how to say it.

Annette stood very close to Sam. Standing beside her husband was where her mother needed to be. They looked perfect together. Her mother's steady gaze and quiet strength calmed Karen's nerves.

Jason should be here with us. For once he'll miss a moment destined to change my life. But any progress will be better than what I had before I came upstairs.

Karen breathed deeply and searched for the right words to say. "Sandy and I came in here to talk to both of you." She pushed out the words that were stuck in her throat. "Brenda saw us in the hallway and tagged along. I'll hurry. Someone is bound to look for us soon."

Annette's lips stretched into a wide grin. "Take your time. Your father and I were on a trip down memory lane. I'm nostalgic over our first Christmas after Jason was born. Your brother's birth completed our family."

"I want him here with us," Karen said, surprised she meant every word.

The glow in her mother's eyes drew her in deeper. Her mom always made her feel loved and protected, specifically during struggles. She rubbed her pinky finger, and hoped for a spurt of wisdom. As teardrops rolled down her cheeks, she focused on the door. Sam quickly gathered his daughter into his arms, and Karen lost the will to run away. Until this moment, she'd steeled herself against him. He'd wounded the family he should have protected. She finally realized the true opposition to her father.

He allowed his wife to keep a traitor as a friend. But Sam was a normal man, with strengths and weaknesses, just like his wife.

While they grew up, Jason had stayed glued to his mom, and Brenda had always favored her dad. But Karen had doted on both parents. She delighted in the time she spent with them together. She'd fallen for their love story and the easy way they communicated with each other. Her parents had perfected how to display affection even when their children were present.

That had been the main reason Karen had dreamed of dating. She couldn't wait to be asked out. It was the prelude to marriage and a family of her own. These days, dating was just the runup to an iffy ever after. What if she chose the wrong man to marry like her mom had done?

Unable to breathe, Karen pulled away from Sam. She retreated to the door, and longed to close it behind her. But she knew she had to stay to correct her part in the friction.

I only have one shot at this reunion thing. I must get my thoughts in order.

She leaned her back on the door. "I hate talking to you all in front of Brenda. Yet, I'm glad she's here. God blessed me with the best sister in the world." She closed her eyes then opened them slowly. "Oh boy. I never expected to have this conversation with my parents." She stared at Sam. "Truthfully, Dad, I want to talk to you without listening to anything you have to say."

Sam reached out his hand. "Karen, please—"

Annette wrapped her arm around his waist when he groaned. "Conversation means that all parties are equally engaged. They both need the chance to speak. If not … it's a waste of time for everyone involved."

"Mom, Sandy instigated this discussion that I didn't want to have. Thank her if it works. Blame me if it fails."

"You have company downstairs," said Annette. "Don't keep them waiting."

Chapter Twenty-Three

Karen began to talk once Sandy touched her arm. "I came to apologize to Dad. Mom, I know Dad loves you, but he messed up big and hid the truth. After the affair, he showered you with love and stability. You felt cherished, I get that. I just can't forget that he left you in a false relationship with Peggy. You thought she was your friend. You treated her special. You let her inside of our house."

There's no excuse for what he did. It was bad enough to have an affair, but it was even worse to leave his wife defenseless with that woman.

She glared at Sam. "Why didn't you protect the woman you love? Mom spent years catering to a woman who'd stabbed her in the back and was still trying to steal her husband."

"I won't refute the charge. I'm guilty." He rubbed his head as if it hurt to think. "There's no defense for cheating on Annette. There's no defense for keeping it a secret, and for allowing Annette to keep Peggy as a friend. I almost lost the woman I love and my family along with her. I handled the situation poorly. I know that. Through the years, I gained insight into my failure and why I dishonored our vows."

His gaze sought Brenda, who stared back at him. "The challenges I faced on the job and at home caught me off guard. The result was my time with Peggy. Fears of losing Annette kept me quiet. I couldn't tell her about Peggy and me. However," Sam said, switching his gaze to Karen, "I—did—not—share—a four-month fling with Peggy. We were together once, which I know is one time too many. I never strayed from my wife again."

Annette laid her head on Sam's shoulder. "Believe him, girls. Peggy alluded to four-months in the letter she sent. After a while she retracted the claim. She's been in love with your father for years. Peggy understands that a relationship with Sam will never happen. That's why she finally gave up and moved away. I can only speculate why she sent the letter."

Sam locked his and Annette's hands together. He brought their joined fingers to his lips. "Karen, I accept the olive branch you brought to me. I understand this visit isn't a cure-all for whatever ails our relationship. But it does present an opportunity to win back my daughter. You've always supported the parent you thought was being mistreated. This is the reason why I never lost hope that our relationship would survive."

He chuckled, and hugged Annette against his side. "Remember, how whenever we planned an outing, but either your mother or I remained at home? You refused to let us stay in the house alone. You faithfully remained with the parent left behind."

Still laughing, Sam looked at his oldest daughter. "Do you remember, Brenda? Your sister never cared about missing out on the treats you and Jason received by going."

"I remember," she said, softly.

Happiness filled Sam's eyes as he turned to Karen. "It's befitting that you sided with Annette over me. I stepped out on your mother. Annette stayed at home."

Karen felt herself relent. "I do forgive you, Dad. I just hate the way things turned out for all of us. Especially for Mom. Peggy is a stumbling block for me. She was a false friend and Mom never knew that Peggy secretly hated her."

Sam's face filled with remorse. His voice sounded hoarse when he spoke. "I won't push you to make declarations you're unable to give. Nonetheless, you girls will never know how much I needed this moment." He hugged his niece on her way to the door. "Sandy, your cousin said that talking to Annette and me was your idea. Thank you for not waiting until morning. Now go back to your friends. We'll talk tomorrow, Karen."

Sandy brushed tears from her lids as Sam sat down on the bed beside his wife. "Karen would've done the same thing for me. She always helps me out whenever I need her."

Karen mopped her eyes with her fingers. She opened the door and peered down the hall. "I must look horrible. First stop, bathroom."

Both girls swung around when her father spoke to Brenda.

"Please, don't go. Stay awhile and talk to us. Your mother and I are wide-awake. Nothing will satisfy us more than a talk with you."

Annette slid away from Sam on the bed. She made room between them. "How about it, love. This talk is long overdue. It'll be a catharsis for all of us. Mainly, for me."

Indecision marred her sister's features. Brenda clearly wanted to stay. She grasped the doorknob and smiled at Karen and Sandy. But her expression showed confusion before she shut the double doors.

Happy that Brenda had decided to stick around, the girls moved away from the door. They practically glided down the hallway with their arms linked together. The cousins were the best friend either one had ever had. In the bathroom, they took ten minutes to make Karen look presentable. They used hot and cold water compresses and drops to banish the red from her eyes.

Sandy talked about Butch as they walked down the stairs.

"Kathy will contact Joey before the game tomorrow. Butch will call you first thing."

Karen uncrossed her fingers. "So soon. You think so?"

"He's hardly shy. Butch pursues whatever he wants: He wants you. That's why he confided his feelings to Kathy. Like him, she never gives up. I'll tell Chris we're doubling up on your second date."

Karen liked the image of Butch and herself as a couple. Especially if his interest was the real thing and not the fickle type. But double dating with Sandy and her boyfriend wasn't on her happy list. She could only tolerate the boy in small doses. Chris was the disaster in Sandy's life that waited to happen.

Excited from the chat about Butch, Karen floated into the family room. Although all the girls wore pajamas, Diane's sleepwear instantly caught her eye. It looked like a bunny outfit that completely covered her feet. The only thing missing was the cute little tail.

"You look so cute. Where did you buy those adorable pajamas? I want to buy a pair for myself."

"I order most of my clothes online. I promised to send everyone a link. I'll send you one, too."

"Karen, sit next to me," said Lisa. She slid over to make room between her and Kathy. She whispered into Karen's ear. "I went to your bedroom, but it was empty. Were you talking to your folks?"

"Yes. We had something important to discuss that couldn't wait until morning."

"Oh. I hope it was all good. I wanted you to come back before I announced my plan." She grinned at Karen when Karen frowned. "It's the youth meeting. I'm going with you on Wednesday. Plus, I'll invite all takers to my house for pizza after school."

Evette lowered her hand from aiming a dart at the dartboard.

"It's about time you did something nice. Yes, everyone, I'm jok-ing."

"That makes three things I know about you," Kathy said. "You have a sense of humor. You can offer sound advice. Plus, you're open to new friendships. What other good qualities are you hiding from us?"

"Are you fishing for information?" Evette asked.

"Um-hmm. It's a habit of mine. Inquiring minds and all of that."

"In other words, she's nosey," said Joann. "Or, what did you call it, Linda? Newsy?" She sighed loudly. "If I can't beat you, I suppose I have to join you. To eat pizza at Lisa's house, nothing more. Pizza next week at a friend's house sounds good to me. I haven't eaten my favorite pig out food in a long time. I'll pass on going to youth meeting with you guys after we eat. Because I overate tonight, and I plan to do the same thing at Lisa's house, I probably should skip Burger Barn tomorrow."

Lisa pouted. "I can't come to Burger Barn. I'll join in the next time we all get together. It'll happen again."

Kathy tossed her slippers across the room. They hit the table, and landed in opposite directions. "Oops. I missed the target. I was aiming for the second shelf." She stretched out on the floor, and wriggled her feet in the air. "Count me in for your pizza party. Are all our friends invited? Or just the people here tonight?"

Karen's stomach knotted into a tight ball. Should she voice her objection or wait for Lisa's reply?

"I think we're building a unique brand of friendship. Why should we repeat the process with newcomers?"

Kathy giggled. "I think I see a trend here. First Karen, and now Lisa. You two are begging to become outsiders. Now for my good idea. What if we each take a turn and supply the meal each Wednesday? I'll go next. In time, we can ask other girls to join in." She turned to Angela. "Is it okay to use food as a witnessing tool?"

"Like Karen used a pajama party?" Linda asked. "She'll probably never admit to doing it. But she did."

Joann laughed. "There's no doubt about that. That's why I refuse to go to her youth meeting. Pizza at a friend's house is okay, but nothing more."

Angela studied the girl who refused to give in. "That's fine. You can always change your mind and come. Join us when you're ready." She let her words sink in and turned to Kathy. "Karen had this sleepover for more than one reason. But there's nothing wrong with sharing your beliefs with others."

"It works as long as no one's emotions get manipulated. That didn't happen here," Sandy said.

"I'm in," said Linda. She looked pleased with herself as she smiled at everyone. "I'll go next after Kathy. Think I'll serve kabobs. I like those. We'll each put in ten dollars once we ask other people to join us. Are you coming with us, Evette?"

"Um, maybe to the youth meeting, but not to eat. It's my job to cook my family's dinner after school."

Diane joined them on the floor. "Come on and eat with us too. We'll have fun. I plan to come *if* my parents let me. Can you cook, Lisa?"

"She makes good pizza," said Kathy. "How will you pull it off? You can't go anywhere if your folks aren't at home in the evenings."

Karen's ears perked up. This was another conversation she'd waited to hear. How her friend planned to attend youth meeting next Wednesday.

Chapter Twenty-Four

"I'm forming a plan," said Diane. "Only, I need my good friend's help to pull it off."

Oh boy, those puppy eyes are staring at me. I won't lie to your parents, even for a good cause, so don't ask.

She leaned forward. "Don't look at me that way. Hear me out before you say no. Every year, I enter the science fair at school. I'll ask to spend Wednesday nights with you so we can tackle a project together."

"There's a reason why I haven't entered the science fair since sixth grade."

"Okay, science isn't your favorite subject. But you ace every class. You're good at science even if you hate it."

Sandy sniggered. "Karen hates losing, not science."

Hesitancy hit Karen as she recalled the losses. "Yeah, all that hard work for third place. It happened three years in a row."

"Geez," said Linda. "Fourth, fifth, and sixth grade. A friend wants you to help her. Just say no if you don't want to do it."

"Then you do it. Since you think it's so easy, have at it."

Linda laughed. "You still have that same awful attitude about not winning first place. I didn't claim that it's easy, only doable—for you. I would help Diane if I knew what to do. You love competing on every level."

"No, I love to win. I no longer compete at science fairs because I lose."

Linda's mouth hung open. "What are you talking about? You took third place every year that you entered the competition. You won, Karen."

"No—I lost. Win, place, or show. I didn't even get second place."

Kathy fell over herself, laughing. "You entered the science fair, not a horse race. So, if you're not number one it doesn't count? Tell that to the ten people who were pleased with their honorable mention. You know you're going to help her. Agree so we can switch topics. I want to know if Evette will come to Lisa's house for pizza."

"Zip it," said Diane. "Wait your turn. We're discussing my social life for the foreseeable future. Karen knows I'm a science freak. How can we lose if we work on the project together?"

Karen perked up. "Think we'll win? You promise? Because if you give me your word I expect to win first place."

"Let's just say we'll have a better chance by pairing up," Diane said. "Teamwork works wonders, or so they say. However, we won't know if it will work unless we do it."

Kathy tapped her heel on the floor. "Are you in? Your eyes twinkled. That's a yes. She'll partner with you." She brushed her hands together, while turning to Evette. "Now, if your mother won't spring you this Wednesday, come on the following weeks. I want you to join us."

"I—I know that we'll have a good time, but, still ..."

"Is there another problem that keeps you from coming?" Angela asked. "Before anyone asks me, yes, I plan to show up." She snapped her fingers. "Oh, yeah, homework. Study class, maybe? I finish most of my projects at school. I seldom have follow-up work to do at home."

Evette shrugged. "I'm booked up all day. No free periods at all, not even on Friday."

Joann stifled a yawn. "Excuse me. It's late, or should I say early. You can't squeeze in homework sometime during the school day? I always do."

"Not if she wants to pass the class," said Kathy. "Tell us the real reason for staying away. Spill it. You've pressed everyone else on things tonight."

Karen squirmed around a little. She hated to see anyone pinned down to answer a question they'd rather ignore. *How can I switch the topic?* About to break in, she waited once Evette spoke.

"Well ..."

Lisa checked her watch. "Spit it out, girl. I'm already falling asleep."

"I—I ... won't have ten dollars to fork over each week. Money is tight in our house."

The conversation faltered when the blushing girl shut down completely. With no explanation, Evette picked a piece of lint off her gown. Her gaze darted to the other girls. Everyone was speechless. Even Kathy and Linda remained silent.

"I feel like a spendthrift," Karen said. She hoped it was the right thing to say. "I waste too much money buying junk food each week."

"I hear you," said Diane. "My father throws money at me, but I can't go anywhere to spend it. I mostly shop online."

"Evette, your problem is an easy fix," said Lisa. "We'll take turns paying your share each week."

"Or, we can all chip in on your part if you don't like that idea," Joann said.

Evette gave a grateful smile. It took a while for her to speak. "Thanks for the offer, but I can't accept. I either pay for myself or

I stay at home. But the youth meeting might be an option I can pull off."

"I know a way you can attend the get-togethers," said Sandy. "Three nights per week I babysit for my neighbor's two sons. I unwisely promised not to quit until she found someone else to watch them. Interested? Please, say yes."

Evette mulled over the offer. "Maybe she already found a replacement for you."

"Uh-uh, no way," said Joann. "Sandy is the only person who would keep those brats."

"Joann! So far, she hasn't had any takers." Sandy smiled at Evette. "Anyway, not yet."

"There is a good reason why that hasn't happened," Kathy said. "Don't listen to Sandy. A wise person will steer clear of 231 Tree Lane Drive."

Karen held her tongue, even though she secretly agreed with Joann and Kathy. Those cute little boys were monsters. Only Sandy and their father could handle the twins.

"Don't listen to them," Sandy said. "I work six to ten Monday, Tuesday, and Thursday. No cooking or cleaning. She pays me two hundred dollars a week to entertain her boys."

Evette's mouth hung open until she snapped her lips together. "You make two hundred bucks to watch two children, twelve hours per week?"

Joann chuckled. "Mrs. Pratt isn't giving away her money. Believe me, you'll earn every penny."

Karen smiled once Evette's lips curved into a wide grin. She had that faraway look like a person who planned to shop.

"Babysitting is a breeze job for me. I'm the oldest of six kids."

"I'm jealous," said Diane. "That's why I adopted Karen's family. Maybe I need close contact with loving people. It's hard to spend so much time alone."

"We adopted you back," said Karen. "Spend the night whenever you like. My mom will love it if you stay over. She's always wanted three daughters. You can spend two nights per week if we work on the science project Tuesday *and* Wednesday." She turned to Evette once Diane agreed to ask her mother to spend both nights. "My father switched careers six years ago. Even though our finances were shaky for a bit, the situation righted itself. I'm sure that will happen for your family too."

"That's true," said Kathy. "No wonder you hated Lisa's sleeping bag remark. I would've hated it too."

Karen almost clamped her hand over Kathy's mouth to keep her quiet. No more looking backwards. The group had finally jelled together. Why throw a stone into the smooth sea of friendship? Her grandmother liked to say, "Let past events remain where they are."

Lisa cringed. "I still feel awful I made that mistake. If I had known in advance ..." She turned to Evette. "What can I say other than I'm sorry."

Kathy tossed a crumbled cup into the wastebasket. Then she turned squinted eyes on Lisa. "Some people refuse to learn the lesson in the first round. Didn't we play out this scene over eight hours ago?"

"Stop babbling. I regret being rude. Okay?"

"Then say that, Lisa, instead of talking like an idiot. Sorry has more than one *meaning*. The word also means wretched, deplorable, and miserable. Is that sinking in this time?"

Sadness highlighted Lisa's features. She nibbled the nail on her index finger. "Leave it to the wordsmith to pick out the negative parts." She touched Karen's hand and tried to smile when Karen did. "I give up being sweet to a person who will never like me."

Kathy held up her hand. "Now I hate you? *That* accusation was hurled nine hours ago."

"But three hours ago, you claimed your life was changed forever, Miss Christian. I knew it wouldn't last." Lisa clamped her lips together and crawled over to where Angela played jacks. Her gaze met Karen's before she picked up the logic problems she'd discarded. "Too bad you folded before breakfast." Abruptly, she put the book aside. "I'm done. No more arguing tonight. Your attitude baffles me. I've always thought we were friends."

Kathy held up five fingers. "For five years. Truthfully speaking, I like you more some days than I do other days. You've had that same effect on me since the first day we met. But I like you."

Lisa flicked her fingers at Kathy. "Stop lying. Who badgers people they like? You find fault with practically everything I say and do."

Karen felt like a ping-pong ball. Her neck ached from looking back and forth between each girl. Somehow it was hard to intervene this time. *Kathy has a lot to say. She may as well say it and get it over with. But how will Lisa hold up under this attack?*

Kathy rose to her knees then sat back down. "Okay, two things bug me about you. The prima donna routine, and the ridiculous way Joann trips over herself to be your friend."

Joann looked startled. "Hey, leave me out of your private war. I don't know what you're talking about."

"Why not? It's easy enough to figure out. Stop running after Lisa. How many times can you say, 'I'll pay your way, Lisa.' As if Lisa can't afford to pay her own way."

"So being thoughtful doesn't work for you? Too bad, I treat all my friends the same way. I'm not a people pleaser."

"You are when it comes to Lisa." Kathy's eyes narrowed as she pointed at Joann. "Starting today, do not call me to go anywhere with you after Lisa tells you no. Why can't you ask me before you get rejected? Call me first. I'm tired of being an afterthought."

"Wait a minute. Is that what you think? Lisa is the first name on my speed dial. After her, I call you. Karen is next after you."

"Did someone else enter the names into your contacts?"

"That's a good point," said Linda. "Kathy, I bet Joann is the first name in your contacts. You've fawned over her from the first day you met her."

"Stay out of this. I have too many friends to *fawn* over any of them."

Linda nodded. "You do hoard people, but you don't count them all as friends. You take relationships seriously. Just look at your family life. Rethink the best-friend thing. You are all friends. No one has to be first over the other."

"Whose reasoning are we using, yours or mine? Only my thinking counts when it concerns me."

Every problem was laid on the table, and Karen hated what she saw. She'd waited five years to hear this conversation. Only, tonight exposed the truth: The girls involved were deeply wounded. There was a huge rift stuck in the middle of their friendship. No more ignoring the inexcusable. Karen wanted the air to be cleared of the bitterness by morning. She was tired of starring in their toxic foursome. Although Linda had tried to squash the backbiting, how would she reply to a darn good question? Karen regularly had ideas about what her friends should do.

"Even though you always butt into other people's business, I'll back off. No, I'm finished," Linda said when Kathy scooted closer to her, and held out her hand. "You and Joann hash it out."

The mood in the room shifted to a place Karen didn't want to go. The atmosphere was stuffy. Time stood still at Linda's and Kathy's deadlock.

Chapter Twenty-Five

Karen waited to see what happened next. Her gaze followed Joann's clumsy movements to the table. She stood there a minute and drummed her finger on a coaster. She crossed to the fireplace before she spun around to face Kathy.

"Look, like Karen said to Lisa, we're friends for life."

She quickly sat back on the floor with the group. "Lisa was the first person I met at Jefferson Middle. She treated me special, and made sure I fit in with her friends." She turned to Linda when Kathy didn't speak. "You remember, Linda."

"Uh-huh, I do. Lisa treated you good on the first day of school. She's never stopped."

"I didn't realize Lisa had a best friend until Karen came back to school the following week. After the first day, I looked forward to being there. I liked you on sight, Kathy. That's why I hung out with you when you came to the school two weeks later. I introduced you to my new friends."

It was amazing how quickly Kathy's resentment seeped away. "Lisa, Karen accuses me of riding you."

Lisa glanced at Karen and then back at Kathy.

"She says it all the time. I always disagree. She was right. I vent my frustrations on you. We're good friends who somehow got off track." She eyed the girl who sat next to her. "You too, Linda. We all got off track."

"Not me," said Linda. "The four of you ran away from me. I was always willing to play ball."

Lisa looked like she wanted to sink through the floor. "That means we all owe you an apology."

"That's right," said Kathy. "I deserted you and then felt sorry for myself." She flung herself at Linda, and hugged her around the neck. "I apologize for walking away from our friendship. There's nothing like seeing who you truly are."

The regret on her face was evident to everyone. She wiped her eyes on Linda's gown. "I don't have a tissue."

Linda frowned at the wet spot on her sleeve. "But you are wearing pajamas." She snapped her fingers. "Déjà vu. Didn't we play out this scene before?"

Karen bounced on the floor. "Oh my goodness. Yes, we did. In this very room. It was at my sixth-grade pajama party. You were there, Diane."

"Aw, yes, I remember. It was Kathy's first night away from home. It was my first time to spend the night away from home, too. But I didn't cry."

"Linda tried to cheer up Kathy," Joann said. "I'd forgotten about the sleepover that year. Thanks for the reminder."

"Forget it. All of you," said Linda. "Let's just start over, beginning tonight. I ... purposely insulted your new friends. I wouldn't let up an inch. I disliked those girls the first time we met them. Seventh grade was a terrible year because they came to Jefferson Middle. Anyway, I kept the hostilities alive on purpose. I forced you all to choose between them and me. Well," she said, playing with a string on her gown. "I ... learned to deal with the loss."

As if on cue, Sandy waved her hand in the air. "We all know adults who failed to grow up. Problems keep repeating themselves until we learn the lesson they bring. My dad told me that. I'd always been guilty of trying to forget my troubles. Despite what people say, everything isn't good, nor is it pointless."

"Me too. I drown out my problems with activity," said Angela. "With that in mind ... Guys, the news is out. Jeff and I split up Wednesday. I won't go into details, although I will admit this: We should've never gotten together. The golden couple wasn't so perfect after all."

Everyone who heard the news for the first time took the information in stride. Compassion flowed to the girl who wore a brave smile.

Joann leaned over and hugged Angela. "That means it's time to move on. It'll be strange seeing one of you without the other. Any guys on your radar?"

"For now, I'm taking a date break. We're not enemies. You'll see us talking."

Joann looked pleased when she grinned. "Good for you. What did you like most about the relationship?"

"That's a good question. Let's see ... hmm." It didn't take her long to come up with an answer. "I liked compromising with Jeff without losing my values to him. I'll be honest, guys. Breaking up with him would've devastated me had we been intimate."

Linda winced. "Believe me, it's not a good feeling. I'm glad you didn't have to go through any of that mess."

Diane nearly choked on her drink. Water dribbled down her chin. Evette patted Diane's back when she coughed. "Ahem," she said. She cleared her throat and wiped tears from her eyes. "You sleep with all those boys you date?"

Linda sputtered as if a lump was lodged inside her throat. She appeared to have difficulty getting her words out. "No! I do not! I have been intimate with my boyfriends. Two boys. Not a football team."

"I didn't mean any harm. I wasn't being judgmental or anything like that." Diane clicked her fingers on her teeth when Linda just stared at her. "I mean, even if you were sleeping around, it would be your business. But I'm happy you don't."

"I second that opinion," Karen said. "Oh Linda, I wish you hadn't slept with any of them. You're much too nice to suffer though that stuff."

Should I say what I really think?

She took a deep breath, and gave herself the chance to change her mind. "The boys you date don't deserve your time. They were all wrong for you. I was happy when you were no longer with them."

Kathy nodded. "Me too. I hate the guys you choose. It's like you scrape from the bottom of the barrel. You deserve much better than any of those boys."

Linda turned away then ran fingers through her hair. "Why not tell me how you really feel? No, no, you're right," she said when Karen said, "Oops," and covered her mouth.

"Here's the truth. The guy I'm interested in won't ask me out. I gave up wishing that he would last summer. I've waited three months for a call from a boy I barely like. He called this evening. But, he's one of the guys Kathy just described. It's good that I had other plans, or I would've agreed to see him."

"Nix him," said Diane. "You already know he's a loser."

Joann patted Linda's droopy shoulders. "Tell us about the guy you wanted to ask you out."

Linda's thoughts appeared to be far away as she squeezed her upper arm. She peered at everyone's faces. "Can you all keep what I say to yourselves? This will ruin my life if it leaks out."

Then she focused on Joann but didn't speak. "This is hard, you guys. I hope I don't regret telling you."

"With that buildup, now I really want to know," said Kathy. "Just tell us who he is and get it over with."

"That isn't your only option," said Karen. "You don't have to tell us anything unless you want to."

"But I will. It's your brother, Joann." Linda relaxed when Joann smiled at her. "Peter talks to me whenever we meet in the hall."

"Peter Conley?" asked Diane. "Lots of girls dream of dating Joann's brother. Me too, but he's never noticed me."

Linda tucked her legs beneath her. "I doodled his name on my hand until a friend guessed the truth. I stopped with the outward signs a while ago. Thinking about a boy that doesn't want you is embarrassing if people find out."

"I know who Peter is," Evette said. "He definitely stands out in a crowd. Girls watch him wherever he goes."

"I know," said Linda. "That's part of the problem."

"Kathy and I see Peter looking at you. He's quite obvious about it," Karen said. "Plus, the girls surrounding him noticed it, too. You're right, he watches you. Peter heads your way whenever he sees you."

"Make a wise decision going forward," said Kathy. "People are watching to see if you and Peter get together."

Joann glanced at Kathy. "Meaning what? Choosing the right boy to date is always a wise thing to do. My brother is a nice guy."

She turned to Linda when Kathy just looked at her. "I'm curious. Do you ever see Peter outside of school? At parties, or at your favorite hangout spots other than Burger Barn?"

Obviously perplexed, Linda shook her head. "Why does that matter? We hang out with different crowds."

"Exactly. Peter doesn't think you share the same interests."

"So why does he always talk to me? What does he say about me? Has he thought about asking me out?"

"Uh-huh. It appears that way to me. Now, how to proceed behind the scenes. Hmm ..."

Joann snapped her fingers. "Got it! Okay, spend this weekend with me. That way Peter can approach you without other people being nosey. He probably won't be at home Saturday night, but he will be there all day Sunday. Especially Sunday night. Curfew and all of that. My dad reins Peter in on Sundays. He'll be a captive audience for the day."

Linda bounced up and down on the floor. She couldn't stop grinning. She was so happy that all the other girls became happy too. "Oh ... my ... goodness! I can't believe I have a chance with Peter! Am I dreaming? Don't pinch me, Kathy. Okay, calm down. I can't," she said, giggling again.

Then she turned serious. "Joann, can—can I trust you to keep everything between *us*. I mean—if he finds out ..."

Joann shrugged. "We'll set the stage and see what happens. Relax, I won't tell Peter. I think he knows you like him. Boys usually think that every girl wants them. I already talked you up when he asked about you."

"I can't believe you're so excited," Diane said with a laugh. "Everything is going to work out fine. For you ..."

"As it will for you, too. Lots of changes are coming for all of us. Your parents will come around."

"Like for Kevin and me," said Lisa. "I think he's history."

"Good riddance. He's okay for someone else," said Joann.

"I'm still surprised that Joann and Peter discussed me," Linda said.

"I do have my discreet moments. Are you still worried about me telling Peter?"

"Linda, you can trust her," Lisa said. "She won't rat you out. Um—I'm glad I only kiss Kevin. I think sleeping with a guy makes breaking up harder to do. Revisit the sleeping-with-your-boyfriend angle."

Her voice lowered, and Linda leaned in to hear. "I think you want a steady boyfriend. Don't forget, Peter and Joann live different lifestyles. He sleeps with the girls he dates. Peter has never had a girlfriend."

Linda hid her face in her hands. "I can't talk about this, not in front of everyone. It hurts too much."

"It will continue to hurt if you don't adjust the way you do things," Kathy said. She did everything except wag her finger. "Peter is cool. But he *knows* he can pick and choose the girls he dates. Protect your heart. He's far from being perfect."

Linda tapped Karen's ankle. "What do you think?"

"That you should listen to wise advice. Peter doesn't play by the rules. He pushes the limit and you only pretend that you do."

"Listen to your friends," Joann said. "My brothers have two sets of rules. One is for their baby sister, and the other one is for the girls they date. Having four older brothers took away the male mystique. Plus, I get a heads-up on every guy that asks me out. Each one understands that if I'm mistreated, they'll deal with my brothers. Always protect your own interests. I'm not talking about safe sex, either."

"I get the point, you guys. I'm listening to every word you say."

"Seriously, Linda," Joann said. "My mother taught me not to let men use me for sex. It's a discussion we've had since I was ten. Those talks are imprinted on my brain cells. Too bad they never swayed my brothers regarding the girls they date. My dad gave them mixed messages. His dialogue with them contradicts the conversations he has with me."

"I won't blow off anything said tonight. I'm taking it all to heart."

"Good. I don't want my friend to get hurt by my brother's lack of respect."

Tears flooded Linda's eyes. "Friends. I like that word. Especially as it pertains to us. It reminds me of old times."

Karen smiled to herself. She liked their relationships getting back on track. This was everything she'd hoped for, plus a whole lot more. Everyone seemed to be on the same page. It was almost time to go to bed. She stifled a yawn, and laid her head on Sandy's shoulder.

"Will your mother allow you to spend the entire weekend with Joann?" Evette asked.

"Do I need to ask for you? I should've asked you that," Joann said. "I will, if it helps. My mother says an automatic no if someone else asks her anything for me. I have to ask her everything myself. But your mom may be different."

"Our mothers are friendly. I'm sure Mom will say yes without a problem. Let's meet at Burger Barn so I can pick up Evette. My treat," she told Evette. "You can buy the next time we go. It's okay," she said when Evette frowned. "I'll let you spend your babysitting money on me."

"Thanks. I've never gone to Burger Barn before. My family ate lunch at The Main Street Diner after church one Sunday. The whole complex is awesome. Imagine five restaurants linked together. We didn't have anything like that in Wichita."

"I can't wait to hang out at The Teapot next year with the college crowd," said Angela. "Their menu is awesome." She yawned, covered her mouth, then she prodded Karen with her fingers. "Wake up. I wondered why you were so quiet."

Karen rubbed her eyes. She lifted her head off Sandy's shoulder. "I'm not asleep. I've heard everything."

"Good, because I'm etching this day on my forever list. God is the real force behind this sleepover. Just look at the revelations we uncovered without even trying. I understand you all, and myself, better—much better."

"Yes!" said Karen. She wrapped an arm around her cousin. "My mom says, 'Jesus is the gift that gives.' "

"We'll never be the same again," said Kathy. She winked at Karen, then swung around, and grinned at Lisa. "All in?"

The girls stretched out their hands, and stacked one hand on top of the other. "All in," they said together. Then they all fell over, laughing.

Diane sat up and checked the clock on the shelf. "It's three o'clock! I can't believe it's that late. Bedtime for me. I have to plead my case to my parents tomorrow."

"Me too, I'm tired," said Sandy. "Karen! We forgot the sleeping bags."

Chapter Twenty-Six

The cousins hurried out of the room but returned in record time, loaded down with the remaining sleeping bags and multiple pillows that were in the foyer.

Then all the girls sprang into action, and spread out across the space.

Sandy and Angela settled in the alcove beneath the window. Linda and Joann selected a spot beside each other against the wall. Lisa nudged Karen and pointed to a space across the room. Karen trailed behind her, but took cover when a pillow whizzed over her head. She removed her arms from over her head when she didn't get hit.

Her eyes narrowed at Diane. "It's too late to have a pillow fight. Half of us are already lying down."

Diane giggled loudly, then bopped Evette on the top of her head with a pillow.

Although she was surprised by the attack, Evette swiftly beat her down. Diane squealed and ran around in circles before she hid behind Lisa. Lisa scrambled out of the sleeping bag and fell into the wall as she struggled to get away.

Karen, awed by the tussle, retreated across the room. She watched the takedown from a safe distance. Evidently Diane had challenged Shiatown's pillow-fight champ. Maybe having five younger siblings meant Evette engaged in weekly pillow wars and won.

Once the drama stopped, Karen kicked off her slippers, and placed her sleeping bag next to Lisa's. About to lie down, she saw a figure enter into her peripheral vision.

Oh, no, Diane, you can't be serious.

About to lay back down, Lisa watched Diane squeeze her sleeping bag in between hers and Karen's. Content with the layout, Diane crawled between the flaps. She placed an arm across her face.

With her hands on her hips, Lisa glared at Diane while Diane drifted off to sleep.

Although most of the girls missed the incident, Kathy and Evette stood to the side. They watched the scene unfold.

Oh no. Which Kathy is looking? The problem-solver or the girl who loves to rile Lisa? Just when I thought we were home-free, Diane did it again.

"I'll handle this," Kathy mouthed to Karen. She ambled across the room, gripped Lisa's hand, and urged her to lie down.

Karen relaxed once Lisa nodded. But she covered her eyes when Lisa kicked her foot over Diane's head as she slid into her sleeping bag.

Karen glanced around the room. The night had finally ended. Nine girls were scattered across the space. No one had defected. They all were still here. Her guests would remain until morning. Each girl lay quietly talking, or simply falling asleep.

Only Kathy and Evette crept about the place wide-awake and giggling.

The girls stood by the fireplace, and chomped on potato chips and popcorn until they moved center stage. Then they placed the purple sleeping bag beside the gray blankets and continued to gab.

Kathy sat on top of her sleeping bag. "It's you and me. I'm glad you're babysitting for Mrs. Pratt. That means you can eat dinner with us after school on Wednesdays."

Evette sat down and scooted closer to Kathy. "You sound sure that I've got the job, but she hasn't hired me yet."

"Trust me, she will as soon as she meets you. Don't worry. You'll start work next week, I'm sure. Hang out with us Wednesday. Lisa makes terrific pizzas."

"I'll plan to eat dinner at Lisa's and go to the youth meeting with you all. With luck, I'll find a way to finish my homework during the week."

"Shh, don't let Karen hear you say 'luck.' She hates to hear anyone use that word. Forget about that. She did say the youths have sixteen classes to choose from. Maybe we'll discover a common interest and join the same class."

"It will be perfect if it works out that way for us. I'm sick of just existing. I want to live again."

"Live again? What do you mean?"

"I've been out of sorts since summer. My best friend stopped talking to me before I left Wichita."

Karen gripped the edge of the sleeping bag to keep from sitting up.

Only Evette would give details when I'm too sleepy to listen. That's okay, I can wait until Kathy draws out everything worth hearing.

She squinted her eyes to see the girls' facial expressions better.

"Why?" Kathy asked. "Is it because you were moving to another city?"

Evette tried to smile, but it failed. Her mouth just looked crooked. "No, she got angry at me for something else." She studied Kathy with a pleading expression. "I went to the movies with her ex-boyfriend before I left the city."

Kathy gazed Karen's way. "That could do it. I wouldn't want any of my friends to date Joey. Even if I stopped speaking to him, which I won't."

"I don't think it was wrong to go to a movie with him. But she got mad and refused to listen to anything I tried to say. She still won't talk to me. I just want to forget about what happened and move on. Maybe I'll tell you about it sometime."

"Only if you want to talk about how you feel. I don't expect you to dish out private details about your life. I seldom do, and neither does Karen."

Karen clamped a hand over her mouth to keep from interrupting. Evette went to the movies with her best friend's old boyfriend.

She wasn't apologetic about backstabbing her friend. What had made her do something so drastic? How could she date a boy her best friend still had feelings for? An old boyfriend, at that. Did she think moving to another state made it okay? Her exit from the city made it even more important that the girls parted as friends. What about Chris? I'm sure she likes Sandy's boyfriend. If it was up to me, she can have him.

Karen peeked through her fingers until she saw Joann tiptoeing across the floor.

"You guys left the lights on. I won't turn off the recessed lights," Joann said. "Kathy, turn off the lamps when you lie down."

Joann snapped off the switch, and pattered back to her sleeping bag. She touched Karen's foot with her toe as she passed by. She whispered to Karen. "Getting an earful? Me too." She said in a louder voice, "I enjoyed being at your pajama party. Thanks for saving a slot for me."

"Me too," said Linda. "How did you pick us, anyway? You did a good job."

Karen's laughter filled the quiet room. "I asked the people dearest to my heart."

"Good answer. This game-changer ended on a high note for me. I'm ecstatic. Goodnight, all."

Each girl said goodnight except for Angela and Sandy.

Linda slapped her hand on the floor. "Are you asleep over there? Goodnight, all!"

"Not anymore," said Angela, as she turned over. "Night-night, Linda. Is anyone else still awake? We'll reminisce over breakfast in the morning. So go to sleep if you are."

Sandy laughed. "Be nice. If you can't make them go to sleep at least you can make them angry, huh? We'll probably eat breakfast at lunchtime. Oh no. I forgot I'm taking pictures of the swim team today. Oh well … I'll get there when I get there. Good night, all, and to all a goodnight. I heard that somewhere, or something like that."

Swoosh!

The sound of Lisa punching Diane's pillow filled the air.

Karen sat up, and scowled at Lisa, who glared at Diane. Except for her lips bowing into a grin, Diane didn't budge.

"No—you—didn't," Karen said. "I won't feed you breakfast regardless of the time we eat if you don't stop playing and go to sleep."

"She isn't playing," said Kathy. "What's up with you? You lost the right to complain once you lay down."

"So say you," said Lisa. She punched Diane's pillow again.

Diane slowly sat up. She clutched the pillow in both hands. "What, Lisa? It had better be good news."

Lisa sat up with her. "Or, what? It's too late to act innocent, you little conniver. Why did you place your sleeping bag in between Karen's and my sleeping bag?"

No one said a word as the six pillows hurled across the room hit their target.

The fight drained out of Lisa fast. She laughed as she threw each pillow back across the space. She smirked at Diane and lay down, then she flipped onto her side.

Diane lay down too and waved at Karen.

Karen closed the door on the last fight of the night. Soon enough, she would feel the strain of another face-to-face with her father. The start over with Linda couldn't compare to mending the relationship with Sam.

Dad's going to insist on talking everything out as soon as my guests go home.

He won't let her forget about their talk today, nor did Karen want him to. She merely wanted an easy way to get past their current issues. His words had sounded believable in the bedroom. She'd taken the time to listen, and she wanted to believe what he'd said. She loved her father and hated the wedge she'd placed between them.

Karen critiqued each facet of the pajama party. The night's results were a godsend on every level. The high points included the time she spent inside her parent's bedroom.

The right girls had been chosen for the sleepover, after all. Everyone invited agreed with her selections. Better still, they all seemed willing to keep the group intact. At least they agreed to eat a meal together Wednesday evening. Who knew where that interaction might lead each one. Pros and cons had abounded throughout the night. There were many unanswered questions and multiple solutions to be thankful for. She thought about the girls falling to sleep.

Linda was set to date a senior who lived with few restraints.

Diane deserved parents that remembered they had a daughter.

Angela could test the waters with other boys without Jeff hanging around her.

Lisa had promised to cut the ties with Kevin.

Kathy and Joey were about to go public. For real this time.

Who knew the real Evette? Karen didn't.

Joann was either an Ice Princess or a good friend. Which version would they see tomorrow?

Karen watched the night light shining in the hallway. Kathy had turned off the lamps and the recessed lights, but Karen could hear her and Evette as they whispered to each other.

Will Butch call me tomorrow? I'm up for the waiting game. But only with him. Life would be perfect if Sandy replaces Chris with Cody. Cody is the real deal for her.

Three weeks of party plans were finally over. What will tomorrow bring from such a good beginning?

A Note From E. C. Jackson

"The Write Way: A Real Slice of Life" is the slogan on my website and Facebook author page. If every person reading my book feels connected to the characters, my job is done.

Pajama Party: The Story is the companion book to *A Living Hope*. Sadie Cummings wrote this book for the girls of Shiatown. Actually, *Pajama Party* is adapted from the play I wrote many years ago.

One day, while I wrote *A Gateway to Hope*, God spoke these words to my heart, *Pajama Party: The Story*. Another labor of love is completed.

I hope you enjoyed the peek inside the lives of nine girls who stole my heart. My prayer is that they stole your heart as well.

The third book in the standalone hope-themed series is coming soon. Continue reading for an excerpt and book blurb from the first two books in the series, *A Gateway to Hope* and *A Living Hope*.

If you liked reading this novel, please leave a review on the site of the retailer of your choice.

Thank you for your time!

A Gateway to Hope

Twenty-one-year-old Neka is a bit of an introvert, she also happens to be stunningly beautiful. When she discovers her friend James is about to be dumped, she sees the perfect opportunity to escape from her quiet life. Can she summon the courage to leave it all behind?

James Copley comes from a ruthless family. It's rubbed off. Years ago, he disengaged from his brother's smear campaign, but now his father has offered him an ultimatum, "Get married or lose your seat at the table." Plotting to stamp his design on the family business, he proposes to a woman, even though he doesn't love her. But his carefully laid plans start to unravel when she leaves him on the day she's due to meet his family. Could years of planning his comeback vanish with her departure?

A possible solution comes in an unexpected form: Neka. She's not only a friend, but the daughter of his benefactor. And she's right there, offering to support him. But will her support stretch to marriage? He attempts to win her over to his plan but collides with her powerful father who wants to leverage the situation for his own gain.

In their fight for survival and love, they are forced to face some uncomfortable truths. Can they overcome thwarted dreams and missed chances to find true love, or does forcing destiny's hand only lead to misery?

Nikhol Lacey stepped into the muted glow from the wall sconce above the door, grabbed her luggage from the porch, and hurried down the stairs. The path lights cast a shining arc across the yard. Pine scented the air, and fresh-cut grass clung to her sandals.

She sidestepped debris along the footpath to avoid snapping any twigs. To anyone looking, the maneuverings would have resembled a child's game of hopscotch. It seemed like ages had passed, but at last she reached her destination. Lips curving into a fleeting smile, she placed her cases at the cab driver's feet.

After shaking her hand, he lifted the bags. His raspy voice broke the silence. "Good morning ..."

"Call me Neka."

She scooted into the car and eased the door shut behind her. But she froze in place when the noisy driver stomped every twig she had missed and slammed the trunk. Her gaze swept over the second-floor windows. The house remained dark inside.

Good. No signs of movement.

Neka lay back on the cushion but bolted upright when the driver sped away, crunching loose twigs scattered across the road.

She brushed her fingers over her neck and chest and then clung to the front of her T-shirt. Familiar landmarks silhouetted against the dusky morning. She sighed, touching the window as her home faded into the receding darkness.

Regret surfaced. Would her family understand her leaving home without notice? Massaging her right earlobe, she laid her head against the seat.

James needed her. She was the only person able to help him. Finally, someone she cared about required assistance that only she could provide. Tears blurred her vision at the admission that she often felt unneeded. Self-revelation came at a price. Closing her eyes, Neka laid her face into the palms of her hand.

She was committed. It was too late to turn back now.

Lord, help me.

* * *

James Copley stood half hidden in the shadows outside the Tulsa airport terminal. He contemplated the disruption to his plans, sighing as he shoved the cell phone into his pocket. Through the window, he watched a stooped man swishing a mop over the lobby floor.

He jerked around and frowned when a car pulled up to the curb behind him. The taxi dropped off an older man in plaid shorts, who hurried into the building without noticing James's six-foot frame standing to the side.

The stillness shifted. Red and orange lights streaked a pattern across the eastern sky. Dawn hovered on the horizon as the night subsided into a brand-new day.

The quiet June morning sprang alive. Steady streams of cars carrying a bevy of people rolled down the street. A white four-wheel-drive SUV pulled to a stop in the no-park zone. A gray-haired lady dropped off a family of five, and they hugged their farewells. When the SUV drove away, it was replaced by a black sedan. A jean-clad man exited the passenger's seat, laughing as he waved good-bye. Vehicles continued replacing each other in fast succession.

The touching scenarios highlighted his fiancée's absence. Did Teri oversleep or have a car accident on the way to meet him? He rejected those ideas, struggling to remember her travel plans. Had she mentioned who would bring her to the airport? Or had he assumed she'd order a cab as he'd done?

Leaving the milling people, he searched for a secluded corner. The spot he chose placed him closer to the curb, though he remained a great length away from the cars. James was a master planner and detested surprises he didn't spring. Not that he willfully devised sneak attacks behind anyone's back. He just worked overtime to ensure no one else affected him with their unpredictability.

A no-show Teri Campbell dealt a harsh blow to plans he'd thought he'd carved in stone. His mind replayed the strategy he'd conceived four weeks ago. Jaw muscles pulsated as he clenched his teeth and bit down hard. An old sinking feeling rose at an alarming rate and failed to retreat when ordered.

Get a grip, man. You can do this. James was no longer the thirteen-year-old boy with lofty ideas.

He glanced at the clock in the lobby and shook his head. Six o'clock. Their flight would depart in ninety minutes. The cell phone had made it halfway out of his pocket before he realized and pushed it back into place. Knowledge of Teri's scheming nature stopped him from calling her.

Why now? Like most people, he hated fighting a hidden foe. No one could adequately prepare for an unknown assault. Without sufficient warning he was just an unarmed soldier in the midst of battle.

As he forced his back against a pillar, James cringed at the thought of abandoning his plan. A sudden chill struck him, as if a northern wind swirled around him. He willed his mind to focus and weigh the situation. The unfurling trouble begged a response, but the wishy-washy brigade held no sway over him. Once he reached a decision, he stayed the course.

Frowning, he stepped forward to reaffirm his resolve. In spite of Teri's absence, his plans would proceed without another hitch. Snags to his plans didn't matter. After living six years on the periphery of his family, James craved their acceptance more than ever. His life was spartan and geared to obtain his primary goal—running the family company. He closed his eyes but failed to block out the memory: days and nights occupied with endless planning, strenuous labor, and not enough rest in between.

But those times were gone forever. Years of hard work with minimal play had paid off. It was time to return home and prove to his folks that life existed after mistakes and bad decisions.

He relaxed his knotted shoulders. He hadn't spent half a decade spinning a web to see it dissipate without ensnaring its prey because of one little snag. This trip was crucial. A lifetime of professional achievements depended on its outcome. He narrowed his eyes as he considered Teri's inflexibility when they'd spoken yesterday. She'd refused to share a cab with him this morning.

The laughter in her voice when he'd tried to change her mind had riled him. "Believe me, James. Nothing could stop me from meeting you tomorrow. Count on me showing up. I'm coming."

Those words hadn't sounded ominous when spoken last night, but now ...

He ran his hand over the concrete pillar. "Not today, Lord. Not after I gave in to Father's demands."

A maroon sedan swept up to the curb. Teri alighted from the vehicle—sans luggage.

James steeled himself. The woman who'd accepted his proposal four weeks ago glanced around as if admiring the scenery. Her slow gait indicated she expected him to meet her halfway.

Forget that idea. That contradicted the way he'd play her game.

His tensions diminished as she approached. Many years battling his older brothers had taught him that remaining calm despite provocation usually won the victory. She hoped to toy with his emotions. Stiffening, he widened his stance, holding his position until she reached him.

Teri's lips curved into a welcoming grin. "Hello, handsome."

When James remained silent, her ready smile vanished. It

seemed she'd lost composure after he failed to respond to her tease. Her glance flickered over to people yelling good-bye a few feet away, and keys jangled in her hand.

Eyebrow raised, he centered in on the restless movements. Teri brushed a bright-copper hair from her face. Nodding, she studied his features as if seeking out weaknesses.

A slight smile touched his lips at the war of wills.

Her tenacity amazed him. She read him well. Instead of being icy, her blue eyes flashed fire.

"When does your flight leave?" Teri pursed her lips whenever she wanted to drive home a particular point. It removed any thought of convincing her of the immediacy of the situation. "You can lower that one eyebrow. I'm not going with you to St. Louis."

Though Teri appeared to brace for an angry outburst, she couldn't keep the smirk off her face. She rubbed her chin, peeking over her shoulder to where the sedan had once idled at the curb.

In one smooth movement, James gently gripped her arm, pulling the unresisting Teri closer. His gaze never left her face.

"So this is the real James Copley." Locking gazes with him, a thin bead of sweat dotted the skin above her lips. "I thought this engagement secured our future. Yet you refuse to talk to me."

"Why should that matter when you disrupted our arrangement at the last moment?"

"I agreed to marry you in good faith. It would be good for both of us." Tossing her curly hair over her shoulders, she laughed. "But you sabotaged our engagement from the start. Twice my friends spotted you around town with Cynthia Ward."

The jealous act caught him off guard. She was acting like a scorned woman instead of someone who'd traded herself for personal gain. He knew her real motive for agreeing to marry him. At another time, her Oscar-winning performance might've entertained him. But he didn't have time to be amused. The clock in the lobby showed he had less than ninety minutes before the flight left.

Teri tossed her hair again, gathering steam.

"We shared two wonderful years together. But Cynthia Ward? For four weeks you claimed you needed me to secure your place in the family business. You should've concentrated on me. Okay, I get it. Women fall all over themselves to please you." She jerked her hand from his grasp. Sneering, she leaned closer. "Where's that winsome smile now?"

James shook his head, looking at the cabs dropping off passengers. "So, unfounded rumors made you destroy our arrangement. You just brushed me off without notice. What about those two wonderful years you just raved about? Your response to your friends' accusations says it all."

"Why did you take her out?"

He laughed. "That question's a little late. I promised to escort her to three events *before* we got engaged."

Moving nearer, her perfume saturated the air. Her quiet appeal might have weakened a lesser man.

"You could have told me about the previous arrangements. Instead, you allowed me to stew in everyone else's version."

James stepped backward. "I can only fix problems I know exist."

Teri's body went limp until she plastered herself against him.

"I blew it, huh? I guess my emotions went into overdrive." She glanced away, shaking her head. "I let a job promotion replace my desire for us to marry. At the time, it seemed simple—career increased, so James Copley must decrease."

She fingered his collar, letting her thumb brush along his neck.

You can buy *A Gateway to Hope* from your favorite retailer.

More information:
ecjacksonauthor.wordpress.com/books/a-gateway-to-hope/

A Living Hope

It was a match made in heaven. Or so everyone thought. Sadie Mae Cummings is all set to marry her childhood sweetheart, Kyle, when she is assigned to tutor Lincoln, the new college football running back. This sophomore phenomenon has all the girls on campus knocking on his door. But Sadie isn't interested in his advances.

Lincoln's overblown ego doesn't take well to being shunned, and he resolves to make Sadie his own. He pursues her relentlessly, until finally Kyle finds himself shut out of Sadie's life, with their shared future crumbling around him.

After two years, Sadie's relationship with Lincoln ends, and she is left having to put the pieces of her life back together. She desires nothing more than to recapture her relationship with Kyle. He has stayed true to the dreams they had planned together, living the vision even without Sadie by his side.

When she moves back to her hometown, she labors to rekindle their love. But things have changed, and Kyle has moved on. Sadie quickly discovers how hard it is to rebuild burned bridges.

Follow Sadie's story as she fights for a chance to restore broken dreams. Will love endure?

This inspirational romance by E. C. Jackson is book two of the Hope series and is a standalone book.

Restless, twenty-one-year-old Sadie Cummings wiped down the counter space in her small kitchen nook. It was eleven o'clock. Five minutes had passed since the last time she'd checked. Sighing, she fretted about her boyfriend's visit that morning.

"Why does he agree to come over, then not show up?"

In no time, morning had slipped into early afternoon. The breakfast she'd hoped would receive raves from Lincoln congealed on the stovetop. So much for using her cooking skills to entice him. With several swift movements, she scraped the masterpiece into the garbage disposal, fighting to control the uneasiness she couldn't dismiss.

She was an expert at fooling herself and others, but today her mind refused to be pacified. One could only pretend for so long before the bottom dropped out completely. Truth had a bad habit of intruding into fairy tales. Especially when the make-believe stories were about real-life events.

The ringing cell phone grabbed Sadie's attention. That her mother was on the other end was a forgone conclusion. Except for an occasional chat with her younger sister and older brother, the cell phone never rang. These days only her mother contacted Sadie on a regular basis. She peeked at the caller ID.

A moment before the call transferred to voicemail, Sadie snatched up the cell phone, held it against her chest, then gave a cheery greeting. Minutes later, she sauntered through the studio apartment thinking up reasonable excuses to end the call early. Jeanette Cummings expected a good deal more than her middle child was able to give.

Still stumped about finding an excuse to satisfy her mother, Sadie walked around in circles.

"Mother, I'm not trying to hurry you off the phone. I recognize your concern for the Franklins. Our families have been friends for years. It's just ... look ... it's ... mother, I don't have time to talk now."

Sadie picked up twine from the counter and wove it between her fingers. Pulling it too tight, she winced, then unwound it from around her fingers and wrapped it around her thumb.

"I made plans for the day."

Lincoln could arrive any moment. Somehow, she had to quickly end this conversation without hurting the only person who regularly called. Friendships were difficult to maintain these days. And her brother and sister only gave duty calls, then ended the conversation in a snap.

Jeanette sighed loudly. "I would offer to call back at a better time, but there isn't one, is there, Sadie?"

"Mom ..."

Sadie slowly shook her head. Guilt surfaced each time she talked to her mother. Raised in an orphanage, her mother wasn't a clingy parent. She believed loneliness caused people to accept unhealthy conditions that a person who felt treasured might avoid.

"Of course, you're removed from the lives of the families in Shiatown," said Jeanette.

Blowing breath through her lips, Sadie laid her head on the cabinet with more force than intended. Wincing in pain, she rubbed the sore spot. The lull in the conversation helped gather her thoughts as her fingers massaged the painful area on her forehead. She parted her lips, then she shut them in hopes that her mother would continue speaking.

After a long pause, Jeanette spoke with a harsher tone than any she'd ever used with her daughter. "Listen to me. The Franklin family supported us through your father's illness and death. We are burying Pastor Franklin this afternoon. His wife deserves a phone call from you."

She paused before continuing. "Don't forget, Sarah treated you like a daughter. You and Pastor Franklin shared the same birthday. September twelfth is four days away. My friend is burying her husband four days before his fifty-eighth birthday. And ... what about Kyle? He lost his father and inherited a ton of responsibility on top of it. Honey, be the friend that I know you are. Time is slipping away. The funeral starts in two hours."

Sadie stretched her neck from side to side, hanging her head in despair. Lately, her mother had begun to accept her decisions without fussing. However, today she seemed determined for Sadie to send well wishes to a man she'd rather forget. Feeling faint, she squeezed her eyelids together, but all she could see was Kyle's sad gaze begging, pleading with her to choose him over the man Sadie picked.

Instantly, anger rose as Sadie justified that choice. She couldn't back down now. There was too much lost ground and no way to regain her footing. The future she'd hoped for was gone. Somehow the leftovers had to be salvaged into a win or, at least, a tolerable solution.

Eyes darting around the room, she braced against the wall. "Friend? Kyle and I didn't break up as friends. He acted like a judgmental pig; his last remarks were cruel."

Sadie fumed. With one look Kyle had made her feel like trash. Less than the muck beneath his shoes. Disposable at best, and at worse ...

"Sadie—"

"Don't excuse him, Mom. Kyle humiliated me in front of Lincoln." She glanced at her shoes.

And the truth is, I didn't deserve any better.

"Oh yes, Lincoln. The wonder man who is far from wonderful. I hate the way he treats you, honey. All women deserve respect." Jeanette continued when Sadie failed to respond. "So Kyle, the man we expected to welcome into our family, means nothing to you? You can just ignore the difficulties he's facing?"

Sadie rested her forehead in her palm. A magic wand could wave all her troubles away. Too bad real life didn't offer fantasy solutions. No one moved forward without blood, sweat, and tears. But where would she begin? Her mistakes had obscured her direction. She felt like a rudderless ship adrift on an endless sea.

Closing her eyes, Sadie brushed teardrops from her cheeks. "Mother, you don't understand."

"More than you can imagine my dear." She paused. "I admit life was difficult while your father was alive. For too many years, his illness handicapped the entire household. Nevertheless, we raised our children using godly values. Principles I'd hoped would follow you throughout your life."

Her mother's appeal fell on deaf ears. Reason came too late. Values? Sadie had surrendered those beliefs to the unpredictable man who could arrive any moment. Somehow Lincoln had worn down her defenses from the moment she met him. His mercurial personality had kept her off balance from the start. First, he'd downplayed her views, and then he stole her innocence, until finally her conscience hung in the balance.

Wavering, Sadie stared off into space, lowering her voice to a whisper. "No promises, but let me think about it, okay?"

"What more can I ask than for you to do the right thing? I love you, honey. We'll talk later."

Saying goodbye, Sadie made her way to the alcove she used as a bedroom. Her gaze went straight to the high school senior picture she'd once cherished. The one that showed a bright-eyed young adult bent on living out her dreams. The photographer had captured a smiling face that exuded hope for a happy future. The ecstatic senior had been on top of the world. About to embark on a new life, knowing the man she loved adored her in return.

Sadie sat on the floor, studying the photo. Her anticipation rose each time she recalled her life before college. Could it be possible? Might there be a second chance with her childhood sweetheart?

Remorse replaced her anger. Teardrops plopped over her neck and chest. In one regretful conversation two years ago, her relationship with Kyle had ended. Slowly, she shook her head at the self-created havoc. Her foolish decisions had destroyed the relationship with the man she'd never stopped loving.

Since then, multiple bad choices had taken her life in a different direction. But the obsession with Lincoln Miller increased in fervor. All Sadie knew was that she had to marry the man who'd single-handedly wrecked her life.

Her college graduation had offered a chance to walk away from the relationship that should've never begun. Instead of saying goodbye to Burgundy, Missouri, Sadie stayed on. She was determined to make a life for herself until Lincoln finished his senior year at the university. After that, who knew where a pro-football career might take them? Unable to find a job in her chosen profession, she was waiting tables at three restaurants to pay the bills.

But last June, Sadie had invited her mother and eighteen-year-old sister for a two-week visit. She'd had big plans for their arrival, revamping the space she rented from the Sloanes into a cozy home with a cottage feel. And after accepting the invitation, the duo drove three hundred fifty miles for a two-week visit.

Sadie had ticked off the hours until their arrival, happy for the first time in two years. But three days into the visit, they repacked their bags and left the following morning. And all because Lincoln's boorish behavior had finally pushed them beyond endurance.

At first, the surprised Sadie had been happy when he showed up to meet her family. However, ten minutes after arriving he'd revealed the real purpose for coming. Lincoln wanted her completely separated from everyone who loved her. He behaved horribly, sowing discord while smilingly shaking hands. He casually insulted her mother and sister whenever the opportunity rose.

So, Sadie had suggested touring the state to enjoy her family alone. But those plans ended once Lincoln invited himself along on the trip. In three days flat, he'd ruined the relationships she'd hope to rebuild, plus tarnished his reputation in her mother's and sister's eyes.

Although they had left her apartment in a rush, her mother and sister's spring vacation hadn't been an entire bust. After bailing out on Sadie, they took the scenic view home, spending eight days touring Missouri before driving back to Shiatown, Oklahoma.

Sadie remembered her sister's outburst as her mother climbed into the car to leave. Sadie had asked her why they were running out on her so quickly.

"No one's running out on you, Sadie," she said, frowning at her. "Trying to like your boyfriend is exhausting. You chose that piece of filth over Kyle; we didn't."

Sadie's spirit died as she observed the tears in her sister's eyes.

The younger woman grimaced in disgust. "How can you let him touch you?" Rolling her eyes, she stomped to the car, then spun around at the door. "Keep him," she whispered, "but don't inflict him on your family." And then, as if they'd just ended a pleasant discussion, her sister entered the car, swiveled in the passenger's seat, and waved goodbye.

Standing at the curb, Sadie had cried openly. Another lifeline had driven off, leaving her with Lincoln. Her family had brought the only happiness she'd experienced since breaking up with Kyle, and then they deserted her three days later. She was alone again, and it was her fault.

After her family drove off, Sadie saw less of Lincoln than ever before. His usual once-a-week stopover dwindled to the occasional Wednesday evening. Isolated from family and friends who had all stopped calling by now, Sadie depended on Lincoln's company more than ever.

Today, reliving the past depleted her energy. Sadie was already anxious before the conversation with her mother had begun, Jeanette's phone call had unsettled her even more. She walked to the bathroom and took a long look at herself in the vanity mirror, trying to bolster her flagging courage.

Moaning, Sadie tilted her head from side to side. Her sleepless nights had become quite noticeable in bright lighting. Troubled, dark-brown eyes, surrounded by blemish-free toffee skin, stared back at her. What did it matter anyway? Looking her best didn't count anymore. At least not to the man who was late showing up. Nowadays when he paid a rare visit, his gaze flickered across the room instead of centering on her.

Ever since she'd broken up with Kyle, she'd tried convincing herself that she was loved and appreciated. A persistent question hammered her mind day and night: Why had Lincoln stopped even pretending to care? The last time she saw him, her wonder man had smiled into her eyes, and then disappeared for three weeks.

While scouring the city, Sadie had realized he'd covered his tracks because no one knew his whereabouts. In fact, most people she'd contacted denied having seen him around at all. Refusing to search for Lincoln anywhere on campus, exploring off-campus hangouts had turned up nothing. Even his running buddy claimed that he hadn't seen Lincoln in weeks.

When things went wrong, the word lunatic surged through her mind as usual. Her hands trembled as she rested her face in her palms. An intense fear of hearing that word flung at herself always paralyzed Sadie. The fact that no one in her hometown had ever hurled that accusation at her father, at least not that Sadie heard, didn't matter. Young ears often heard words no one spoke out loud. *Sadie Cummings's father is a crazy man, and maybe his daughter is crazy too.*

Oh, Lincoln, please cooperate with me just this once.

She sank to her knees in front of the vanity cabinet. Could two years of servitude end with her prayers unanswered? Had she forfeited the man she loved only to lose the man she left him for as well?

Standing, her gaze darted around the room. She refused to give up. There must be a reasonable explanation for his three-week absence. At least one that she could live with.

Resting her chin on her chest, she considered her options. There was no easy way out of the mess she'd created. Following her heart meant facing Kyle, a man who might hate her. Anyway, her ex-fiancé had left Shiatown for California, moving himself light-years away from past burdens. Available females had flocked around Kyle since his thirteenth birthday. How much more would they swarm the man as he continued to live out his dreams?

God, I won't be able to rise above a rejection from him.

Mind made up, she took a deep breath. Call Kyle? The disgust in his eyes the last time she saw him still haunted her dreams at night. And Miss Sarah, the woman she'd always considered a second mother, must loathe her too. Gasping for breath, Sadie wiped a warm towel across her face. How could she contact the woman she'd ignored since breaking up with her son? It would be much better to express her regrets through a floral arrangement sent to their home.

She stared unblinkingly into space. Unless her suspicions concerning Lincoln were confirmed, she would forgive and forget as usual. How could she give him up? Too much had been lost. Her whole way of life had changed since their first introduction. No other viable avenue existed since she'd burned her bridges behind her.

Staring at her reflection, Sadie frowned at the shadows beneath her eyes. There must be a way to keep Lincoln. She snapped the lid shut on her makeup kit and squeezed her eyelids together. Why delude herself? Somehow, the man she lived for was slipping farther away.

But how do I fix a relationship I simply want to end?

She jumped when the doorbell rang. Should she ignore the person or shoo them away before Lincoln arrived? Walking slowly to the door, she peeked through the blinds.

"Lincoln?" Why hadn't he used the spare key he'd talked her into giving him?

Sadie took a deep breath. Mumbling to herself, "I won't be a pushover," she swung open the door and slammed into a brick wall of resistance from Lincoln.

You can buy *A Living Hope* from your favorite retailer.

More information:
ecjacksonauthor.wordpress.com/books/a-living-hope/

About the Author

E. C. Jackson began her writing career with the full-length play *Pajama Party*. For three and a half years she published the *Confidence in Life* newsletter for Alpha Production Ministries, in addition to writing tracts and devotionals. Teaching a women's Bible study at her church for eleven years led naturally to her current endeavor of writing inspirational romance novels and teen and young adult fiction. Her mission: spiritual maturity in the body of Christ through fiction.